Random carrot

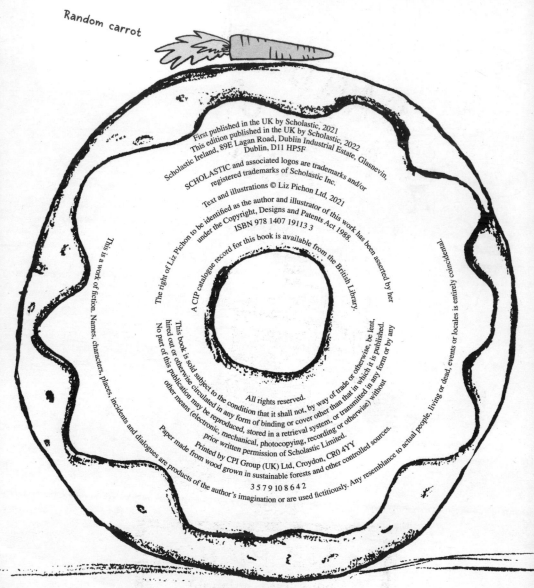

First published in the UK by Scholastic, 2021
This edition published in the UK by Scholastic, 2022
Scholastic Ireland, 89E Lagan Road, Dublin Industrial Estate, Glasnevin,
Dublin, D11 HP5F

SCHOLASTIC and associated logos are trademarks and/or
registered trademarks of Scholastic Inc.

Text and illustrations © Liz Pichon Ltd. 2021

The right of Liz Pichon to be identified as the author and illustrator of this work has been asserted by her
under the Copyright, Designs and Patents Act 1988.

ISBN 978 1407 19113 3

A CIP catalogue record for this book is available from the British Library.

Printed by CPI Group (UK) Ltd, Croydon, CR0 4YY

Paper made from wood grown in sustainable forests and other controlled sources.

3 5 7 9 10 8 6 4 2

This is a work of fiction. Names, characters, places, incidents and dialogues are products of the author's imagination or are used fictitiously. Any resemblance to actual people, living or dead, events or locales is entirely coincidental.

RANDOM ACTS of FUN

Treat

Another random carrot

By Liz Pichon

(who likes a laugh)

SCHOLASTIC

But my IDEA of FUN isn't always the same as everyone else's. 😊

Delia looks like she's having FUN right now.

She's PEERING round the door and smiling at me.

I'm not used to seeing her like that.

"Hands up anyone who'd like a WAFER?" she asks.

(It's stupid question – but I answer it anyway.)

"ME, I DO!"

Delia holds out a wafer in her hand, then

WHIPS it back when I try and take it.

"Very FUNNY..." I sigh.

"I know, isn't it?"
She LAUGHS and begins
to slowly unwrap the wafer.
"HEY! I thought that was for me?"

"I asked if you LIKED wafers, not if you WANTED one."

NORMALLY, I'd just go and get my OWN wafer
from the kitchen,

but I can't, thanks to...

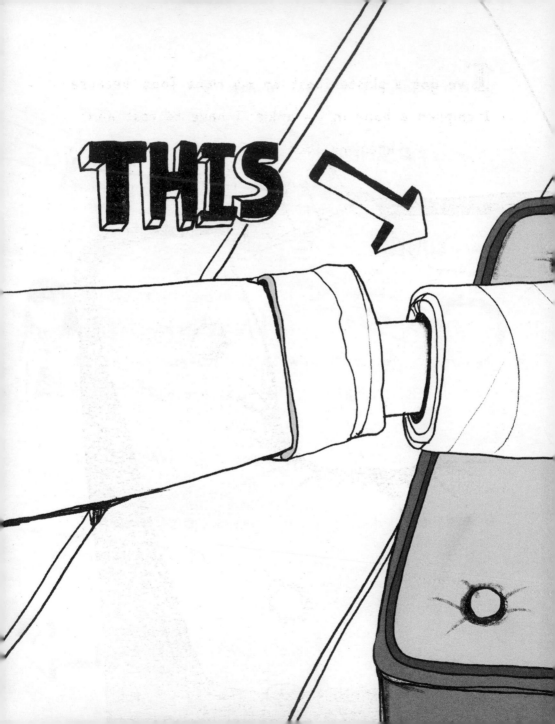

I've got a plaster cast on my right foot, because I chipped a bone in my ankle. I have to rest and keep my foot PROPPED UP on a cushion.

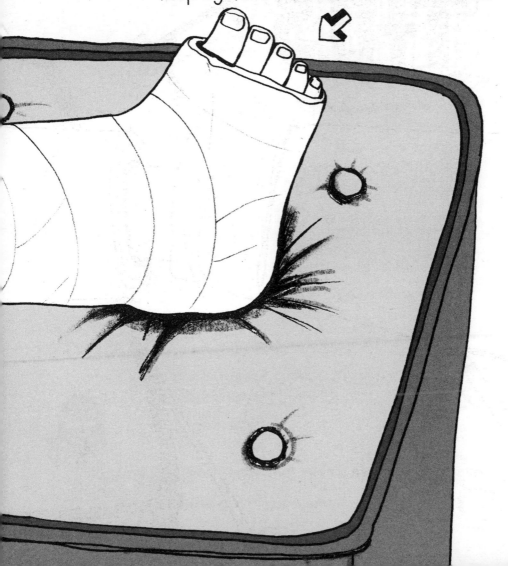

Delia sits down next to me on the sofa and makes me BOUNCE up a little. Then she RUFFLES my hair and says,

"Look on the bright side, Tom – no spelling tests at school for a while." (I hadn't thought of that.)

"Oh yeah," I agree.

"OR, they could send you LOADS of HOMEWORK to do."

Delia makes a point of saying "LOADS" really loudly.

"That won't happen," I say confidently.

"How do you know?"

"Amber Tully Green broke her arm, and she wasn't sent ANY homework," I tell Delia.

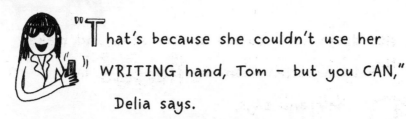"That's because she couldn't use her
WRITING hand, Tom - but you CAN,"
     Delia says.

She seems to be enjoying herself a bit too much
for my liking. She's holding the wafer so
close to my nose I can smell the delicious chocolate.

 It's very distracting.

"Do you want some?" she asks me.

I pretend not to be interested in case it's another
trick question, and shrug my shoulders.

Delia breaks the wafer in two and offers me the
 smallest piece.

    "That's not HALF,"

      I grumble.

  "Suit yourself,"

    she says and goes to eat BOTH pieces.

"OK! OK! I'll have it."

Delia hands it over and says,

"This is **FUN**, isn't it?"

(Not really.)

"Now tell me what happened,"

she adds and points to my foot.

"Isn't it OBVIOUS?"

"Dad said you were <u>IN</u> a **Bakery**.

How do you break your foot in

a **Bakery**.?"

"I was *RUNNING* <u>T O</u> the **Bakery**,"

I explain, because that sounds a lot better than ...

I was JUMPING 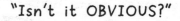 for joy over a doughnut ...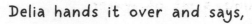

... and I **fell** over my own feet.

As I'm talking, a bit of wafer
goes down the wrong way and makes me cough.

"Do you need some water?" Delia checks.

"Yes - **COUGH** - please. I'd get it myself
- **COUGH** - but I can't move."

"It's OK, Tom, I'll get you a glass of water."
Delia is being nice to me - which doesn't
happen very often. So I'm going to make the
most of it.

Imagine if I had a little
BELL to ring when I needed
something?

Ding DING DING!!

"Delia – I'd love a copy of ROCK WEEKLY, please."

DING DING DING!!

"You can take my tray now."

Ding DING DING!

"I'd love a blanket to warm my foot."

That would be BRILLIANT.

As Delia goes to the kitchen, I call out to her...

"DELIA!
DELIA!"

She comes back in a HURRY.

"What's wrong?"

"Don't worry – I've just found the remote control."

"I wasn't worried, Tom,"

Delia says and gives me a LOOK.

I do another small COUGH ≡3 to remind her I'm STILL waiting for my glass of water.

(Maybe having this plaster cast on will be more FUN than I expected?)

Delia comes back and hands me the water, but it's tricky to drink when you're lying down.

I make a small amount of effort to sit up – then I ask for a straw.

"I don't want to  spill it – thanks, Delia," I say and 😊 smile sweetly.

"A STRAW? Anything else I can get you – a peeled GRAPE, perhaps?"

"CRISPS would be better..." I suggest.

Delia goes back to the kitchen with a HUFF.

"CHEESY PUFFS, PLEASE!"

I call after her, so she knows exactly what I want. 😊

Delia comes back with a /straw, but there's no sign of my CHEESY PUFFS - which is disappointing.

"Oh - nothing to eat?" I ask, then explain WHY I want the crisps.

"Did you know that I collect crisp packets?"

"Yes, Tom - I've smelled them FESTERING in your bedroom."

(I don't know what festering means, but

the way she SAYS it sounds bad.)

Before I can ask her another question, Delia suddenly WHIPS out a pen.

"It's MY TURN to sign your plaster cast."

"Errrr, hang on, NO!" I try and stop her but it's too late.

Delia is already looming over my foot.

 She starts
WRITING.
"Don't touch my toes, I'm
TICKLISH," I say.

The way Delia's LAUGHING makes me THINK
she's drawing something silly.
"There you go – a lovely message from me."
(I doubt that.)

"What is it? I can't SEE."

"It will be a surprise for you,"
she says, which is ANNOYING.
Mum and Dad come and join us, and straight away
Dad asks, "How are you doing, Tom?"

"I'm a bit hungry. Some crisps would be nice?"
 Delia RUFFLES my hair again.
"Good try, Tom."

Mum and Dad ignore my CRISPS comment and
start inspecting my foot instead.

I WIGGLE my toes to get their
attention. Dad TWEAKS my little toe and
makes me JUMP.

 "At least they're all in good
working order."

 "AND talking of WORKING..." Mum adds.

 (Huh?)

"Mr Fullerman has sent a nice message saying
you're not to worry about missing your SHOW AND TELL
or ANY of your other schoolwork."

"I wasn't worried,"
I say, which is sort of true.

In case they've forgotten, I remind them what the doctor said.

"Remember, I <u>have</u> to rest for SIX weeks, and the doctor definitely didn't say anything about work."

SIX WEEKS
– really?

Dad sounds surprised.

They start talking OVER my head, like I'm not even HERE.

"But who's going to be looking after Tom when we're both working?" Mum wants to know.

"Bob and Mavis said they'd help out," Dad says.

Now I'm thinking about my SHOW AND TELL in school.

I don't want to get into TROUBLE.

NOT from Mr Fullerman, but from Delia. I sort of "borrowed" her SIGNED DUDE3 poster to take into school for my SHOW AND TELL ...

Delia's poster

... and LEFT it there.

I need to get it BACK before Delia SPOTS it's missing. But as I'm stuck at home, that's going to be tricky.

While Mum and Dad are STILL chatting (mostly about ME), I turn on the TV to distract myself from thinking about the **BAD** poster situation.

And, YES! I'm in luck. :)

THE JOLLY FRUIT BUNCH is **ON.** (Ha! Ha!)

(My favourite.)

This episode is called:

THE JOLLY FRUIT BUNCH Take A Tumble

As I'm watching ... I realize this isn't going to be the distraction I was hoping for. Oh...

(Hmmm...)

Here's what happened to me

BEFORE the accident or

(B.T.A.)

I'd been SO focused on going to the NEW **Bakery** after school for tasty doughnuts, that I'd ALMOST forgotten it was my turn to do the

SHOW AND TELL.

<u>WHAT</u> should I talk about?

Good question.

I could pick:

①. My EXCELLENT **CRISP PACKET COLLECTION.**

I'd shrunk some of them down to turn into really small badges. They all looked BRILLIANT,

if I do say so myself.

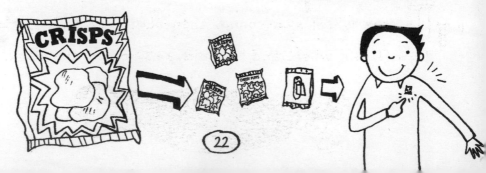

2. THE VERY OLD TOYS.

In really ancient times before there was TV, Mum used to play with these old toys that she keeps in a box.

The teddy has a string in its back that you **PULL,** then in a **growly** voice, the teddy would say,

I'm hungry ... grrrrr...
Will you be my friend?
I'm a bear...
I love HONEY...

I got a **SHOCK** when I first heard it, because the voice sounded just like my Aunty Alice first thing in the morning.

Morning, Tom.

There's also this metal wheel toy that's pretty NIFTY.

You PUSH UP the handle really fast to make the wheel spin round, then BLUE and RED sparks fly off the wheel and it looks amazing in the dark.

3. **OR** I could bring the  poster that was **SIGNED** by **THE BAND!**

I found it in an envelope on Delia's bedroom table.

I don't know why she hasn't put it on her wall.

If it was **MY** poster, I'd be showing it OFF to EVERYONE.

Look at my poster.

I sat and thought about my **SHOW AND TELL** for a very LONG time

Honey, please!

then decided to take the **DUDE3** signed POSTER (and the crisps for BACKUP).

My plan was to "borrow" the poster and bring it back the same day, that way Delia would have NO IDEA ...

that it was GONE.

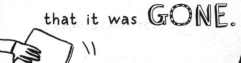

Delia not missing her poster

I'd tell everyone in my class all about how **AMAZING DUDE3** are.

DUDE3 are so-so.

Marcus would probably disagree –

but then he'd be wrong (obviously).

All I'd have to do is AVOID bumping into Delia so she wouldn't start asking awkward questions like:

"Is that MY POSTER you've taken?"

"How many crisp packets do you really need?"

I slipped the envelope with the poster inside under my sweatshirt, and squashed the crisps into my bag.

Then I walked past Delia CONFIDENTLY. "🖐" She l👀ked at me and said NOTHING. (PHEW.)

I WAVED bye to Mum and Dad, then went to meet Derek, who was waiting to walk to school together as usual.

The first thing he said was: "I can smell CRISPS."

"It's my crisp packet collection for **SHOW AND TELL.**" I opened my bag to show Derek, and he nodded his approval.

"That's **GENIUS**, Tom. Do you remember when Rooster was MY **SHOW AND TELL** in school?"

"How could I forget?"
The whole school talked about nothing else for WEEKS after Rooster's visit.

"Everything was fine until the last lesson before lunch. Mr Keen was heading to the staffroom with a sandwich in his hand...

He popped in to say hello to Rooster, who thought the sandwich was for him."

"It's an easy mistake to make if you're a dog," I agreed.

"I've never seen Rooster jump that high or run through someone's legs so fast," Derek reminded me.

"Rooster SURPRISED a lot of people that day. Even Mrs Mumble got a visit," I told Derek, then LAUGHED.

It had taken Derek **AGES** to get him to come back.

Rooster was having too much **FUN.**

EVERYONE wanted to bring their pets in after that. At the next school council meeting, Pansy suggested we have a

BRING YOUR PET TO SCHOOL ☺ DAY. Mr Keen said, NO.

(Not surprisingly.)

Instead, he put up a **PET HALL OF FAME NOTICEBOARD** where we could pin PICTURES of our pets up.

(Which wasn't the same thing at all.) 😗

Right now, it's covered with pets that I'm not sure actually EXIST. There's a picture of a tiger, a shark and a woolly mammoth. Even Mark Clump doesn't have a pet like that.

(Or does he?)

Back to the **SHOW AND TELL.**

Most of the kids in my class had already done theirs. Although Julia Morton had forgotten it was her turn, Whoops... and when **M**r **F**ullerman asked her to start, she just GRABBED the FIRST thing on her desk.

A pencil case.

"Off you go, Julia – tell us ALL about your pencil case, then," **M**r **F**ullerman told her.

(I wasn't convinced <u>this</u> **SHOW AND TELL** was going to be very interesting.)

"I keep pencils in my pencil case..."

(No kidding...)

"And pencils are USEFUL for drawing

... keeping hair out of my eyes ...

(?)

... and you can knit with them too," she explained.

(Really?)

30

At this point, Marcus put up his hand and announced to the class, "Tom can knit – can't you?"

"Oh, yes – you can!" AMY had joined in. "Errr sort of, only a scarf, though. My granny taught me," I tried to explain while Julia demonstrated HOW to use a pencil to hold UP her hair – it worked too!

"That's not something <u>I'll</u> ever be able to try, Julia," Mr Fullerman had joked, pointing to his BALD head.

Then Julia had showed us some of her drawings, which were excellent. It was impressive how she had come up with ALL those things to do with pencils so fast.

Pansy Bennet was up next.

"**T**HIS is a Venus flytrap – and it EATS flies," she said.

Straight away, we **ALL** had questions to ask.

Will it eat your finger?

Or your whole hand?

HOW **BIG** does it grow?

Where can I get one from?

Do they come from SPACE?

Pansy answered most of the questions, then took out a small dead fly to demonstrate how to feed it. The two sides of the spiky flower head slowly curled together to

TRAP the fly inside.

Close-up

Woooooooooooooooooo.

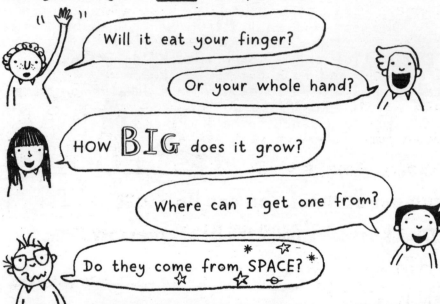

EVERYONE wanted a Venus flytrap after watching that. (It's on my birthday list already.)

Pansy's **SHOW AND TELL** was going to be a hard act to follow. But **DUDE3** are an excellent band, and I <u>knew</u> Delia's poster would be a good way to start telling the class how AMAZING they are.

I stood up and took out my envelope, and was ALL READY to go when **Mr Fullerman** said,

"Sorry, Tom, we've run out of time! You can do YOUR SHOW AND TELL tomorrow."

"OK, sir, I'll be ready," I told him and immediately got <u>so</u> EXCITED about going to the **Bakery** that I left the poster behind. (I'm hoping Delia won't NOTICE it's missing YET.)

"TOM - did YOU take an envelope from my bedroom?" Delia is staring at me STERNLY with her arms folded.

(Uh-oh...)

I point to my foot.

"Errrrrrrrrrrrr, how could I?"

"BEFORE you did that. It's got something very special inside."

"I don't think so,"
I tell her, keeping my eyes on the TV.
"Right - you won't mind if I take a look in your room, then?"

"Go ahead," I say confidently, because I know it's at school.

Delia STOMPS upstairs and I can hear her opening drawers and searching around my bedroom. I just hope she doesn't find anything else I might have borrowed.

NOW feels like a GOOD time to do some doodling and IGNORE the sound of Delia searching.

I'm going to draw something on my plaster cast.

After all, I've got six WHOLE weeks to FILL it UP.
I'll draw something *FUN* (and delicious).

Like THIS

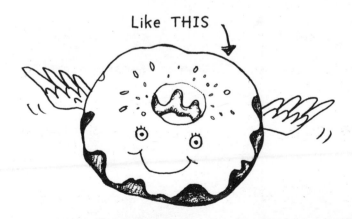

A flying

(I can't stop thinking about doughnuts.)

DOUGHNUT DOODLES

It's been a few days now since the accident and I'm SAVING this space on my plaster cast for my friends to ADD their messages and drawings when they come to see me.

Space

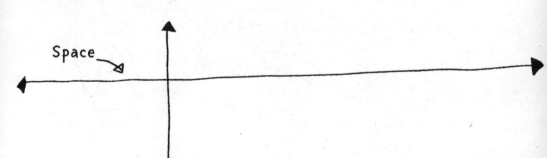

There's loads of blank pages to FILL up in my notebook too. I'm trying to keep busy, and so far doughnuts feature a lot.

I'm **NOT** OBSESSED with them.

(Maybe a little.)

I like other things as well. ☺

Carrots are nice.

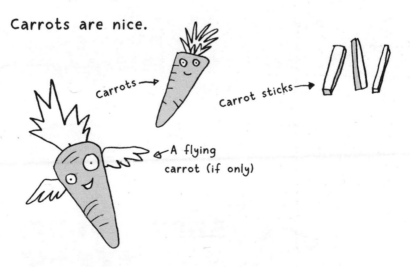

Carrots →

Carrot sticks →

← A flying carrot (if only)

Here's a poem I wrote ALL **A**BOUT...

 CARROTS ~~DOUGHNUTS~~

A Poem About Doughnuts

By Tom Gates
(who likes doughnuts)

To the doughnut

I am devoted

Full of jam

And sugar-coated

Eat them slowly

Don't be hasty

SOFT and **FLUFFY**
Nice and **TASTY**

38

If **YOU** don't like

Delicious DOUGHNUTS

YOU'RE a doughnut.

The End

Here's a story about ...

~~CARROTS~~ DOUGHNUTS

(and bugs)

By Tom Gates

Once upon a time there was a little green **BUG**, who only liked to eat doughnuts. Green Bug liked them SO much, he'd eat one whenever he could.

The other **BUGS** would tell Green Bug:

"You can't live on doughnuts alone — you need to eat your vegetables and other food that's GOOD for you!"

But Green Bug wouldn't listen to ANY of the other bugs AT all.

He thought he knew BEST.

(This was NOT true.)

One day, Green Bug discovered a **Bakery** bin where a lot of old doughnuts had been thrown out.

"This is a DREAM! I'm going to eat them ALL."

Don't!

yelled Stripey Bug,

or you will TURN into a doughnut.

YIPPEE!

Doughnut BIN

"What a load of old RUBBISH. I can do what I want – so THERE," Green Bug said RUDELY.

Then he CHOMPED his way through all the doughnuts until ...

... they were all gone.

Green Bug felt a bit sick and had to lie down and have a rest.

"I'll sleep if off and will feel FINE in the morning," Green Bug groaned.

Stripey Bug shook his head.

"I'm not so sure," he said.

It was a long night. Green Bug didn't sleep much. There were a LOT of noises going on in his tummy.

The NEXT morning, when he woke up, Stripey Bug was STILL there, looking stern.

"I knew this would happen!" Stripey Bug grumbled.

Green Bug HAD turned into a doughnut.

"I'll have to ROLL you everywhere now!" Stripey Bug began to PUSH.

"Whoops," Green Bug said.

"I'll never eat another doughnut again."

(Until next time.)

The End

Here's a few more drawings and doodles featuring...

~~CARROTS~~

DOUGHNUTS

Doughnut Mum

Doughnut
Delia

Doughnut
Marcus

← Bits of
sugar

Doughnut Mr Fullerman

Mrs Nap
Doughnut earrings

Doughnut
Rooster

Doughnut
Skateboarding
Monster

(Enough about doughnuts — for now.)

Here's a FACT I found
out about carrots...

The LONGEST carrot
ever recorded (not in
a singing way) was
over 5.7 metres
long or 19 feet.

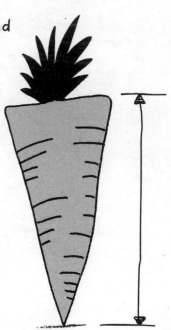

(Back to my ANKLE.)

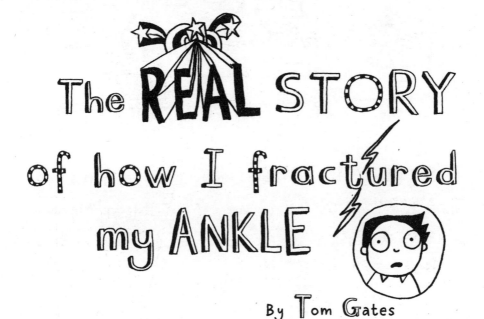

The REAL STORY of how I fractured my ANKLE

By Tom Gates

(a very brave person)

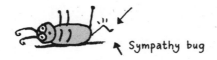

← Sympathy bug

Marcus Meldrew sits down next to me in class and I notice his face is covered in SUGAR (like the drawing I did).

It's on the TIP of his nose, his chin and above his lip like a sugary moustache.

I <u>COULD</u> tell him, but I decide not to. His face might cheer me up during the MATHS lesson. Marcus will have no idea why I'm looking at him and smiling.

"What's so FUNNY, Tom?" Marcus wants to know.

"Nothing. I'm just in a very good mood," I say.

"It's maths now, so that won't last."

"**M**aths is OK. Besides, I've got something else to cheer me up," I add.

"**I'm** in a good mood too you know," Marcus says and gives me a **SUGARY** smile.

 "Why's that, Marcus?"

"I went to the NEW **Bakery** before school to get a **TREAT** for my lunch. But I couldn't WAIT, so I ATE it. You'll NEVER guess what it was."

(His sugary face makes more sense now.)

"A ?"

"How did you know?"

"Because I'm really smart, Marcus."

"**And** you've got sugar all over your face," **AMY** says, which sort of gives the game away.

Marcus uses the back of his hand to wipe away the sugar – then LICKS it.

"Do you HAVE to?" AMY asks, not looking impressed. It's the SLURPING noises he makes that are really bad.

"YOU'D do the same – it was the BEST caramel doughnut I've ever had."

"DID YOU JUST SAY CARAMEL DOUGHNUT?"

I repeat.

Suddenly, I'm very interested.

"Yes, they do lots of different flavours in the new **Bakery.** Chocolate, banana, strawberry, sprout."

"Huh?" "What?"

"That's a joke, Tom.

No one would eat a sprout-flavoured doughnut."

"I wouldn't," **AMY** tells him.

(I agree with **AMY**.)

"HOW did I <u>NOT</u> know about this Bakery?" I say
LOUDLY enough that **M**r **F**ullerman hears me.

**"Today we're doing
FRACTIONS in MATHS, so
you can pretend to be
DIVIDING up a CAKE from
that new Bakery, Tom.
Which IS very good, by the way."**

(Dividing a cake would be the easiest fraction ever.)

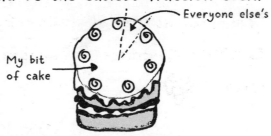

Everyone else's

My bit
of cake

53

"**M**arcus is <u>right</u> – they're the <u>best</u> doughnuts EVER. I like the jam ones," says **AMY**.

She's AGREEING with Marcus, which doesn't happen very often.

I can't wait to tell **D**erek about this **Bakery** at break time. He really needs to know all about this

IMPORTANT DOUGHNUT NEWS!

YES!

"I've been there already, Tom. Didn't I tell you?" Derek says.

"I don't think so..." I reply.

Then Solid says he's tried every flavour of doughnut, and Leroy loves them ALL.

I love them ALL.

"They're DELICIOUS!"

Florence has been there twice. Norman wants doughnuts to be our new band practice snack. Even the little kids playing CHAMP know what their favourite flavour doughnut is.

Jam   Banana   Toffee   Lemon!

I feel like I'm the ONLY kid in the WHOLE school who didn't KNOW about this Bakery.

I HAVE to TRY one of these doughnuts for myself to see what all the FUSS is about.

"LET'S GET DOUGHNUTS AFTER SCHOOL TOMORROW," I shout and Derek sighs.

"Calm down, Tom – I've gone right off doughnuts..." he tells me, which is a **SHOCK!** Huh?

(Derek waits a few seconds before saying...)

"**HA! HA!** I'm joking, of course I'll come!"

For a moment I thought he was serious!

NEWS of our **Bakery** TRIP spreads SUPER FAST around all our friends, and the rest of the day, I'm finding it hard to concentrate on anything ELSE.

EVERYWHERE I LOOK, ALL I CAN SEE IS DOUGHNUTS

I see them when I
get home too.

I EVEN see doughnuts when I get ready for bed
and close my eyes to go to sleep.

AND when I OPEN them in the morning too. Only it's Mum wearing her new glasses and telling me to get up.

I can't stop thinking about the **Bakery** now.
At breakfast, I ask Mum and Dad a very
important question.
"How do you feel about **DOUGHNUTS**?"

"They're fine for a treat, Tom, but an
apple's better for your packed lunch,"
Mum says, almost guessing my next question.

"I used to buy apple doughnuts from the **Bakery**
when I was a kid," Dad tells us, combining the
two things nicely. So I try again.

"Can I have a tiny bit of money to go
to the **NEW Bakery**, because <u>all</u> my
friends are going and EVERYONE in the
WHOLE ENTIRE SCHOOL has tried the
caramel doughnuts?" I ask them hopefully.

Mum and Dad keep me waiting...

"Caramel doughnuts..." Mum repeats slowly. Then surprisingly, they say YES and give me enough money to buy FOUR doughnuts.

"That way you can bring them home and we can ALL try one, Tom!" Dad tells me and rubs his hands together like he's excited about the doughnuts.

"BUT ... what if I want to eat TWO?" I check, as it's a STRONG possibility.

"Just don't," Mum warns me.

(Worth a try.)

As well as being excited about doughnuts, it's also MY turn to do a **SHOW AND TELL** in class. I've already worked out what to talk about.

(Delia's **DUDE3** poster and my crisp packet collection.)

The poster's hidden under my sweatshirt, the crisp packets are in my bag, and **NOW** I've got doughnut money too. **TODAY** is just getting BETTER and BETTER!

In school

I'm all SET for my SHOW AND TELL in class when Mr Fullerman says, **"Sorry, Tom,"** because we've run out of time and I'll have to do it the NEXT day.

This is NOT a problem for me.

At least NOW I can fully focus on

The **Bakery** is very close to school, so it won't take long to get there either.

There's a NICE BUNCH of us all going together.

IT'S EXCITING.

Solid, Norman, Florence, Leroy, AMY, Derek and Marcus are just as KEEN as ME and looking forward to trying different-flavoured doughnuts THIS MUCH.

Then Marcus says,

"You know we should really get a move on,

or the **Bakery** might run out of caramel doughnuts."

 WHAT?

That's when the walking stops,

and the *r u n n i n g* starts.

As we turn the corner, in the distance we SEE a

BIG group of children from GREAT MANOR

SCHOOL, and they are all heading towards

the **Bakery**.

"Oh no! Those Great Manor kids don't mess around,"

AMY tells us.

"They might buy ALL the DOUGHNUTS and

there will be NONE left for us,"

Solid shouts, adding to the *PANIC.*

Marcus yells, so we run even *faster*.

The Great Manor kids can SEE us running and they

start to run too.

"FASTER!" I shout.

We all get to the **Bakery** at the same time.

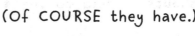

"Calm down, you lot! One at a time!" the **Bakery** staff tell us.

Somehow, the Great Manor kids have squeezed in FRONT of us.

(Of COURSE they have.)

"This is going to take **AGES** now..."

I grumble — but not loudly enough for any of the Great Manor kids to hear.

Marcus shouts from the back of the queue, "Are THERE ENOUGH CARAMEL DOUGHNUTS LEFT?"

"I think so!" I shout back.

"I LOVE DOUGHNUTS!" Leroy calls out.

Then we watch as each kid takes a really **LONG** time deciding which flavour they're going to try.

We all watch like HAWKS as each doughnut is carefully placed into a box and neatly tied up.

 (I just want them to **HURRY UP!)**

When it comes to my turn ... I'm like a coiled *spring.*

I hand over the EXACT
money for four caramel doughnuts.
I can't WAIT to try them.
I've already picked out which one is going to be <u>mine</u>.
(The BIGGEST, obviously.)

I tell everyone I'll wait outside so someone else can get their doughnuts. I feel so HAPPY about finally having a caramel doughnut in my hand that I do a small...

LEAP of JOY

Somehow I manage to LAND in a very awkward way.
My foot bends and my ankle wobbles as
I fall over. I watch in SLOW MOTION as all
the doughnuts fly out of the box.

Noooooooooooooo.

I SQUEEZE the doughnut I'm holding so tightly that it

EXPLODES

EVERYWHERE.

STICKY caramel flies through the air. Some of it only goes and LANDS on a Great Manor girl's schoolbag. She quickly brings out a WET WIPE, <u>scrapes</u> it off and throws it in the bin in one EXPERT NINJA move.

(Great Manor kids are always prepared.) Unlike ME. I'm still on the floor, and now my ankle feels like it's on FIRE.

Marcus comes out of the shop and looks
at me on the ground. "What are you doing, Tom?"

"Ummmm – having a rest," I tell him.

"YOU DROPPED your doughnuts,"
he says, like I did it on purpose.

"It was an accident, I fell over," I mumble.

(I don't know WHY I'm explaining myself.)

Then the Great Manor kids gather round me and STARE.

Derek moves everyone away and tries to help me up.

"Are you OK, Tom?" Solid asks.

"My ankle hurts, I think I'm fine though," I say, trying
to stand up.

I'm still holding the squashed doughnut in my hand.

(Bits of it, anyway.)

"You're not going to EAT that now, are you?"
a Great Manor girl asks me.

"No, of course not. It's squashed," I tell her.

(I admit - the thought <u>did</u> cross my mind.)

 I try and stand up, but I can't move my ankle.

My friends are being helpful and Solid offers me a bite of his doughnut.

"No thanks," I say.

Derek knows something is SERIOUSLY wrong when I say **NO** to a bite of doughnut.

"Your ankle is looking pretty **PUFFY**," **AMY** tells me.

"I think I should call your parents, Tom,"

Derek says, and I nod.

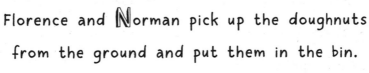 Florence and **N**orman pick up the doughnuts from the ground and put them in the bin. I hand over the remains of my doughnut too. It's a VERY VERY sad moment. **D**erek calls home and Mum says she's on her way.

"You might have to go to the hospital,"

AMY tells me.

I really hope NOT.

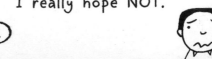

Mum arrives, takes one look at my ankle, and, with Solid's help, they get me to the car ...

... to hospital.

I've only gone and **broken** a bone in my ankle.

 Oh...

I'm going to need a plaster cast on my  FOOT.

When the doctor first told me, I was almost excited (I've never had a plaster cast before). UNTIL she said I'd have to keep it on for ...

SIX WEEKS.

You'll need it for six weeks.

"When exactly do you think Tom can go back to school?" Mum asked the doctor.

"After his next check-up – he'll have to rest for a while first," the doctor told her.

(I liked the REST part.)

"Six weeks..." Mum repeated slowly.
Then suddenly I thought about all the **FUN**
things I was going to miss out on with a
plaster cast stuck on my foot.

NO going to Leroy's swimming party.

No school trips.
No running, jumping, climbing trees,
leaping from the stairs,
throwing and catching my frisbee.

Six weeks feels like a very long time to me too now.
Once the doctor put the plaster cast on my foot,
we were allowed to go home.
I was very quiet — for a change.

(I might have been thinking about doughnuts too.)

When we got back from the hospital, Dad ran out to meet us and helped me out of the car.

"TOM! Are you OK?"
he wanted to know. Mum and Dad watched me wobble around the house trying to get used to holding the crutches the hospital had given me.

"At least I'm only missing school and not something REALLY important - like a holiday," I tell them both.

"That's one way of looking at it, Tom," Dad LAUGHS.

Mum was already making suggestions for FUN things to keep me busy over the next few weeks.

(SIX to be precise.)

"HEY, TOM! You can help me sort through that box of old photos. It's the perfect job to do sitting down with a plaster cast on," she says.

"TV's good for that too," I point out.

"Granny and Granddad can come over and keep you company while we're at work," Dad lets me know.

"And don't forget Delia will be around too," he adds, like that's a GOOD thing.

"IF I had a DOG, I wouldn't be on my own and I could train it to bring me treats, which would be very handy right now," I remind them both.

"**Y**our granny will bring you treats!"

Mum reminds me.

 "That's what I'm worried about..."

"We'll find ways for you to have **FUN** without

a dog, Tom. The SIX weeks will **FLY** by,"

Dad says, then does a *whoooshing* sound effect.

whooosh

"I hope so," Mum says quietly.

"I'm going to make the most of my time by

doing lots of drawing, doodling, reading

books and **comics** and filling my notebook up,"

I tell Mum and Dad.

"It'll be **FUN** to hang out at home and RELAX,"

I say, then YAWN and drop my crutches.

Getting ready for bed takes longer than it normally does. And sleeping in a plaster cast is a bit awkward too...

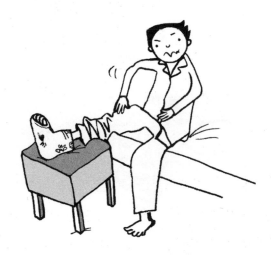

I have a dream that my foot gets stuck in a
GIANT CARAMEL DOUGHNUT
and I can't pull it out, so I have to EAT it.

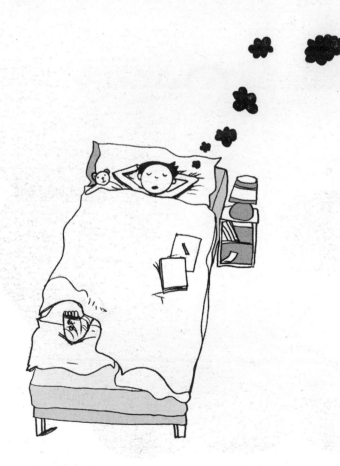

RANDOM FUN
with THE FOSSILS

Delia has just left for college, and Mum and Dad are getting ready for work, when Granny and Granddad arrive to keep me company.

We're here!

"Great timing, Mavis and Bob. You're the dream team!" Mum tells them while bundling up some papers into a folder.

That's when I realize that Mum's working in the living room today – and I can't watch TV.

This is quite annoying.

"Tom's got some school worksheets to do, so you could help him with those today,"

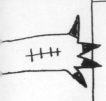

Dad suggests before heading off to his shed.

(Even more annoying.)

Dad points to a small pile of paper that
Mr Fullerman has *sneakily* emailed overnight.
"Don't forget what the doctor said – I need to rest,"
I remind everyone, in case they've forgotten.

"We'd love to help with your work, Tom,"
Granddad tells me.

"Let's have a look,"
Granny says, and they each pick up a
worksheet and have a READ –
then put them back down.

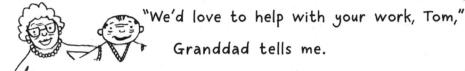

"Haven't a clue,"
Granddad says, shrugging his shoulders.
"Let's do something else for now," Granny suggests.
I AGREE.
Granny has knitted me some FOOT warmers
that will help keep my toes snug.
They look surprisingly stylish, I think.
This one's a **MONSTER.** ➡️

This is a funny shark.

Bug on an island.

Foot warmer with eyes.

Granny's also brought some weird-looking buns too.

(They're a FUNNY colour with black bits in them.)

While THE FOSSILS have some tea and a weird bun, I show them the drawings I've done on my plaster cast. It's a good way to avoid trying a bun. For SOME reason, it starts off a whole BIG conversation about what they were like as kids, which I wasn't expecting.

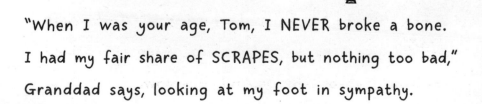

"When I was your age, Tom, I NEVER broke a bone. I had my fair share of SCRAPES, but nothing too bad," Granddad says, looking at my foot in sympathy.

"You've been very brave, Tom," Granny tells me.

"Yes, I have."

"I never broke any bones, either," Granny continues.
"I had a few bumps and bruises – but that was all."

"What sort of things DID you both get up to, then?" I want to know.

"Well, with NO TV in the house, I'd play in the streets with my friends and we'd make up our own games," Granddad tells me.

"Whoa... NO TV?" I repeat, letting that sink in.

"We'd take turns to hold a piece of wood like a ramp on the floor, then the other kids would lie on the ground in a row..."

And then we'd cycle as fast as we could to JUMP the ramp and over all the kids underneath. We'd be like **DAREDEVILS** on our bikes!

"Wasn't that really dangerous, Granddad?"*

I say, sounding like a grown-up.

"I did CRASH once! And knocked out a tooth

– when I had real teeth."

Granddad GRINS and points to his mouth.

(Then Granny joins in...)

"I lost this tooth when I was younger by rollerskating down a steep hill and forgetting how to stop."

She shows me her tooth as well.

It's a FAKE tooth.

* Yes, it is dangerous.

"That reminds me!" Granddad says.

I used to play bat and ball with my friend Paul. He'd throw the ball up in the air to hit it ... MISS ... and get me instead. I got a black eye once – it was an accident, but Paul's nickname was "Rotten Shot" for a reason.

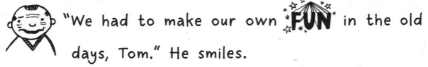

"That sounds AWFUL, Granddad!" I tell him.

"We had to make our own in the old days, Tom." He smiles.

"Getting a black eye doesn't sound like fun to me," I point out.

"I used to play LEAPFROG with my friends going to school, which was FUN," Granny says.

"Until one day, I didn't LEAP high enough..."

...It wasn't pretty.

AGH!

Granny and Granddad are having a GREAT time remembering their **SCARY** childhood games.

Just when I think they're running out of **BAD ACCIDENT** stories to tell me, they think of a few more.

I used to play football at school when the balls were made out of leather. My friend Robert Wong kicked it at me in the rain, so it was WET and **HEAVY.**

OOFFFF

It sent me FLYING.
We did laugh!

Granddad remembers.

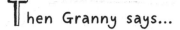
Then Granny says...

What about the time I jumped off a swing and landed – WALLOP – right in a bunch of stinging nettles. AGH

Ha! Ha!

I used to climb trees in the park, and once I FELL OUT on to the ground with a THUD. Couldn't dance for a while after that. OW!

Granddad does a little shimmy to demonstrate.

"All we're saying, Tom, is you really need to be more careful! We don't want you hurting yourself or breaking any more bones," Granny and Granddad tell me. Then they pick up a pen each and add their names to my plaster cast.

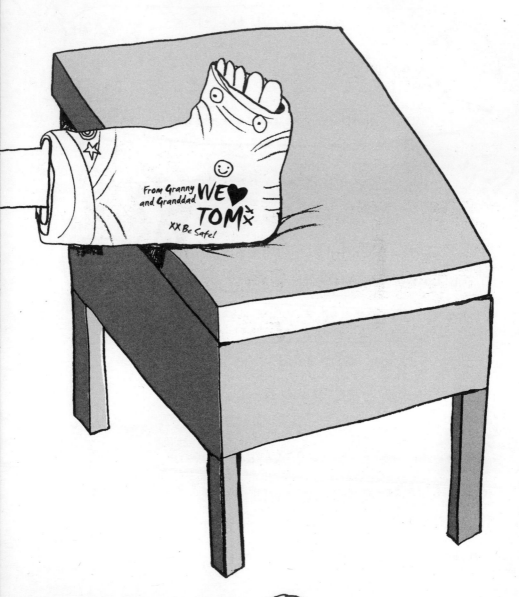

MY GRANDPARENTS ARE LEGENDS.

RANDOM FUN
WITH FRIENDS ☺

The novelty of having a plaster cast on my foot is wearing off a bit. I'm getting fed up with not being able to do what I want. Like getting into the bathroom FIRST.

Delia can hear the

CLONK... CLONK... CLONK...

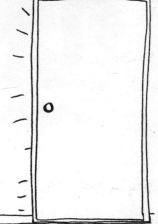

of my plaster cast and keeps nipping in before me.

My morning routine goes something like this now:

)) Scratch my toes.

Wait for Delia to get out of the bathroom.

Hop downstairs to have breakfast.

Listen to Mum and Dad discussing what I'll be doing today.

Nod in agreement. "

Make my own plans.

Choose a window to look out of and use my notebook to write down interesting things that are happening.

WAVE at Derek as he's leaving for school.

SHOW him a FUNNY drawing

I've done to try and make him laugh.

(He does! ☺)

One of my neighbours saw my drawing the other day.

She wasn't that impressed.

Derek liked it though.

Granny and Granddad have been coming over most
days and bringing me BRILLIANT things to keep
me busy, like this thousand-piece jigsaw puzzle of
a very 𝔽𝕃𝕌𝔽𝔽𝕐 cat.

It's going to take a while to do.

Before jigsaw   After jigsaw

They've also given me a paint set, some old **comics,**
and a few packets of SEEDS to plant as well.

"How long do they take to grow?"

I wanted to know.

"A few weeks, that's all," Granny told me.

"They're called mustard and cress and you can put them in sandwiches and eat them," Granddad explained.

 Normally I'd pick that sort of thing OUT of a sandwich, I thought to myself.

"They're DELICIOUS! You'll see," Granny said.

The first packet I tried sprinkling on a flower bed – which was a mistake. The birds flew down and ate all the seeds in five minutes FLAT.

The other packet I put in a pot that I
drew Delia's face on so that when
the seeds grow, it will look like her HAIR.
I can't WAIT. ☺

I showed her my handiwork to see what she thought.

"Do you like it? It's you with plant hair," I said.

"Oh yes - that's hilarious, Tom," she told me
WITHOUT smiling.

(Secretly she was excited... I could tell.)

A BIG package has arrived this morning with
my NAME on.

"It's for you, Tom," Mum says and passes it over.

I'm really EXCITED to see what it is!

Maybe my OTHER grandparents (The
Wrinklies, I call them) have heard about my
accident and sent me something nice in the post?

I hop over on my crutches...

"Oh." It's ANOTHER school project from Mr Fullerman for me to do. And a Get Well Soon card from my class that they've all signed. Some kids have drawn pictures too.

From Marcus

Your face being sad

GET WELL SOON from class 5F

"What have you got there?" Mum asks.

"A get well card and a few worksheets," I say really quietly.

"Did you say WORKSHEETS? We can help you with those." (Mum has superhuman hearing.) "You don't want to fall behind," Dad tells me and picks up my worksheet. They both STARE at them for a very long time.

"Do you understand this?" Mum asks Dad.

"Nope, haven't got a clue."

They both look confused.

"**D**erek will know what to do – I can ask him over to help," I suggest and Mum and Dad think it's a very good idea.

Good idea.

It'll be nice to see **D**erek. We probably won't spend too long on my worksheets. I haven't seen many kids from school yet – I think everyone's busy. I've been trying to keep busy as well. I've been looking out of different windows and watching the world go by, then writing things down in my notebook.

TOM's NOTE BOOK

Me writing interesting things down

There's a tabby CAT who lives in the house across the road that I've never noticed before. It likes to climb the tree and *SNEAK* into <u>other</u> people's houses!

I <u>wonder</u> what it gets up to?*

Bandit (our supply teacher Miss Gravel's dog) comes for walks up our road during the day... ON HIS OWN (Who knew? Not me, that's for sure.) I got excited when I saw Bandit.

Mr Akedo, the man who lives opposite, is learning to drive. He's not very good at parking yet – it takes him a long time.

Big space

Mr Akedo

On the pavement

*See page 230 to find out more

I've spent a LOT of time
watching Mr Akedo in his car.

It's a bit like a real-life videogame.

Here's a picture of a BIRD I saw that was very
colourful and made a lot of NOISE.

Red

SQUAWKING

SQUAWKING ← LOUD

Green

I've NEVER seen one
like this before. I
wonder what it is?*

FACT

The bins get picked up on Monday.
I've taken to waving
to everyone and saying HI
because it's exciting and I
haven't been out much.

*Find out on page 233

This is a picture I'm going to show Derek tomorrow.

I think he'll like it.

Meanwhile, here is an update on my plants.

RANDOM ACTS OF NUF

(fun backwards)

Derek and I have been making up games to play from my window. This one's good.

We write words BACKWARDS like THIS

SDRAWKCAB
BACKWARDS

And then the other person has to work out what it says and write it down SUPER FAST or they lose.

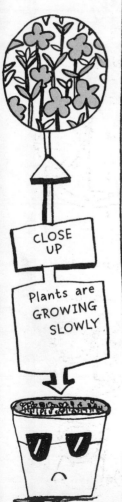

CLOSE UP

Plants are GROWING SLOWLY

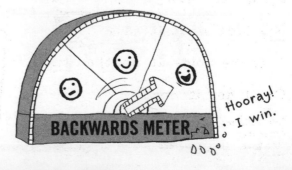

BACKWARDS METER

Hooray! I win.

RM NAMRELLUF
SI A TUNHGUOD
(Clue)

Like this*

and this

RETSOOR**

I EVOL
LEMARAC
SREFAW***

Derek thinks we should make up our own language so we can write messages to each other and no one else will understand. He holds up a sign to show me, and I have <u>NO</u> idea what it says.

Then he holds up another sign...

Oh, I get it now.

s'ti a
EKOJ****

*Mr Fullerman is a doughnut
**Rooster
***I love caramel wafers
****It's a JOKE

UNEXPECTED FUN

(Or DETCEPXEnu NuF...)

Looking out of my window (where I get a good view), I can see the neighbour's tabby cat has gone up the tree again. One of the things the cat likes to do is SHAKE the LEAVES on the branches. I couldn't believe my EYES! The cat waits until someone is walking underneath, then SPOOKS them by shaking the leaves so they fall on their heads.

I'm SURE the cat's doing it on purpose.

As I'm busy watching the cat, I suddenly notice something else that's UNEXPECTED.

BANDIT is walking down the road with a WHOLE loaf of bread in his mouth. I TAP on the window to TRY and get his attention, but Bandit doesn't hear me.

I shout, "BANDIT! BANDIT!" but he is busy with the bread.

I try and RUN downstairs as fast as I can go (which is still not easy to do). But by the time I stumble to the bottom of the stairs, Bandit's gone. Delia's in the kitchen and comes out to see what the noise is.

"Did you fall down the stairs?" she asks.

"Nearly..."

"Don't fall down the stairs, Tom," is Delia's advice to me.

(At least she doesn't mention her missing poster...)

I keep on Delia's GOOD side and say,

"Yes, Delia..."

By the time I get to the front door, Bandit has disappeared down the street.

"Awwwwwwwww, I MISSED him," I say.
Mum hears me and thinks I'm talking about Derek.

"He only lives next door, Tom.
You can ask him round."

"No, Bandit, the sausage dog. And THAT cat is up the tree again, shaking leaves," I explain.

"How are the worksheets going?
Have you done any?" Mum wants to know.
I hobble into the front room and pretend
I didn't hear the question.
Mum follows.

"Oh look, there's Mr Akedo. He's having another driving lesson," I say, changing the subject.

"He has to park the car now – and that always takes ages. I've watched him go up on the pavement before," I tell Mum, who sits down next to me.

"I wonder when his test is? I'll pop a card over to him if he passes," Mum says, getting comfy.

"Might be a while yet," I add, as we watch Mr Akedo go backwards and forwards, trying to park.

"I can't watch," Mum whispers, peeking through her hands.

"I could WAVE at him again – it might help. I waved the other day too, just to give him support."

"I'm not sure WAVING will help."

Mum moves the curtains to one side so we can both get a better view.

"He's going to do it, fourth time lucky.
Oh no – wrong angle." Mum is getting drawn into my world.

"I'm looking forward to taking my driving test.
I'd be a **GREAT** driver," I announce.

"What makes you think that, Tom?"

"By the time I learn to drive, cars might be able to drive themselves, or even FLY in the air."

"Not soon enough for
Mr Akedo, though!"

Mum says as he tries to park again.
"It's rude to stare," Mum tells me, while staring.

"**P**oor Mr Akedo – I think he's just hit the lamppost."

(He has.)

I wave at Mr Akedo to show support. "When did you take your test, Mum?" I ask her.

"As soon as I was eighteen. I passed first time – unlike your dad. **U**ncle **K**evin took a few goes as well. Your dad loves to remind him of that. Come on, Tom – this is painful. We can't keep staring out of the window."

We watch for another ten minutes and cheer when Mr Akedo finally manages to park.

Hooray!

"Let's go - we've got things to do, haven't we?"

Mum tells me. She stands up to leave - but then

I spot a squirrel.

"LŌŌK at that squirrel, Mum!"

I say.

"Come **on**, Tom - it's just a squirrel.

You've seen squirrels before."

"This one's holding something and it's digging up the

garden!" I tell Mum, and suddenly she's interested.

"WHAT? WHERE? HEY, that squirrel's

eating my BULBS!"

Mum bangs on the window to try and scare it off.

It doesn't work.

"I think it's WAVING at you,"
I tell Mum helpfully.

 "Cheeky squirrel – it's like we've opened a
squirrel takeaway! I wondered what happened
to all the flowers."

Mum isn't happy and *BANGS* on the window again.

 "*GO AWAY!*" she shouts.

Mr Akedo stares up at us.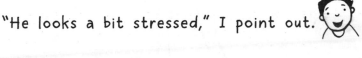

 "NOT YOU, MR AKEDO – the SQUIRREL!"
Mum shouts some more.

"He looks a bit stressed," I point out.

"I know how he feels – I'll have to go down
and chase that squirrel away. It's not
LISTENING to me."

"It's a squirrel, Mum, what do you expect?" I say.

(111)

I get to stare out of the window a bit longer, as I have the best view of Mum chasing the squirrel away. I take out my notebook and write...

Squirrel 1 - Mum 0

As soon as Mum leaves, the squirrel comes back and takes the rest of the bulbs. I make a quick correction in my notebook.

SQUIRREL ~~1~~ 5 – Mum 0

RANDOM ACTS OF PHOTO **FUN**

After all the squirrel action this morning, I agree to stop staring out of the window and help Mum sort out the old photos. *Oh look there's a car...*

"This is very helpful, Tom. When you're finished, you can do one of your school worksheets," she tells me.

"OK – but this might take a while," I say. I'm already thinking I can make this job last for a very L O N G time. Mum shows me the albums and explains what to do.

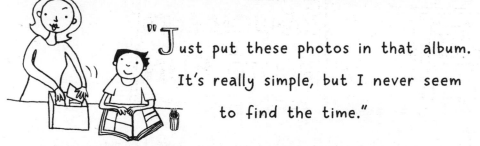

"Just put these photos in that album.
It's really simple, but I never seem
to find the time."

"It's all that squirrel chasing you've been doing,"
I remind her.

"And I have to explain to Mr Akedo that I
wasn't shouting at him. At least the
squirrel didn't come back." She smiles.

(It did – but I keep quiet.)

"Can you just write in that space who's in the
photo or where it was taken and when while I make

a few phone calls."

Mum shows me what to do.

"I won't be long," Mum says
and leaves me to it.

This job turns out to be a
lot more FUN than I expected.

I begin by looking at the photos and picking out the ones I like. Then I think of FUNNY CAPTIONS and write them on bits of paper.

Like this

When you think your lesson's over, but it's only been five minutes.

Before your parents realize the superglue is missing.

When you know you'll never be the favourite child.

That moment you discover the good snacks.

When you think no one knows you broke the vase and blamed your little brother.

I have a lot more  **FUN** than I expect sorting out the photos and adding my HILARIOUS "EXTRA" commentry before lunch.

Mum seems impressed and gives me some GOOD NEWS. "Well done, Tom, and guess what? Your dad went to the new **Bakery** this morning."

I STOP what I'm doing and get excited. If it wasn't for my plaster cast, I'd be jumping for JOY.

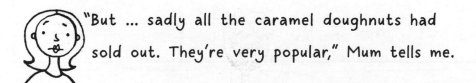

YES

"But ... sadly all the caramel doughnuts had sold out. They're very popular," Mum tells me.

(My doughnut JOY didn't last long.)

Oh...

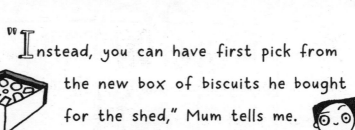

"Instead, you can have first pick from the new box of biscuits he bought for the shed," Mum tells me.

It's not exactly the same, but after a very **long** and careful LOOK, I pick the foil-covered orange biscuit.

The good thing about this biscuit is you can make a small foil CUP afterwards.

(Well, that's what _I_ do.)

I present THIS foil cup to me...

(Another way to pass the time and put off doing my worksheets.)

Here's some more things I made with FOIL...

FUN WITH FOIL

Foil MONSTER

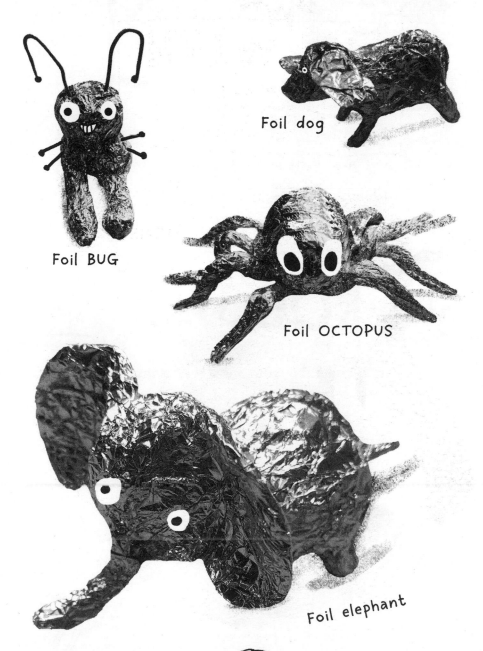

Foil dog

Foil BUG

Foil OCTOPUS

Foil elephant

RANDOM ACTS OF ROOSTER

I've not had any visitors for a while, and then all of a sudden ... Derek, Leroy, AMY, Florence, Norman, Marcus, Solid and

ROOSTER?

ALL come to see me after school.

IT'S THE BEST NEWS EVER!

WOOF

Rooster gets a bit overexcited, so Mum asks us to go in the garden.

woof
woof
WOOF

woof
WOOF
woof

Delia's upstairs too, and I can already hear her sneezing. (She's allergic to Rooster.) It's a nice day and the garden looks lovely, so we don't mind going outside.

My friends take turns to inspect my plaster cast and want to ADD to the doodles on it.

"Your sister's written a nice message," AMY says. "Really?"

I'm about to ask WHAT it is, when Delia pops her head out of the kitchen door.

"PLEASE keep Rooster in the garden, will you?" she shouts.

Rooster hears his name and goes to say hello. Delia closes the door until he goes away

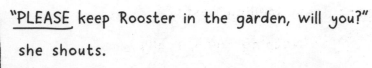

– then opens it again.

"And can you tell Mr Fullerman that Tom needs MORE homework to keep him busy?" she tells my friends.

They all STARE at her and don't know what to say.

"Do you really want MORE homework?" Florence checks.

"No, that's my sister's idea of a joke," I explain.

"Your sister's funny. I like her sunglasses,"

AMY tells me, because she doesn't know my sister.

"She's not THAT funny," I say, then change the subject. "What have I missed at school? Apart from spelling tests."

"Nothing much, really."

Derek shrugs his shoulders.

"You missed the trip to the toy museum!" Marcus adds.

"Oh – I'd forgotten about that."

(I really wanted to go as well.)

 "It wasn't THAT good, Tom," Leroy tells me.

"Well, I enjoyed it," Marcus adds.

"I'm sure we'll go there again," Florence reassures me.

 "I hope so. It was really .

Marcus is a bit keen to let me know.

"Can I have a go on your crutches?" Norman asks me, so I let him.

"It was Mr Sprocket's birthday the other day, Tom," Norman tells me.

"Was it?"

"Yes, it was brilliant. He gave everyone in assembly a sweet," Marcus pipes up. "Before the show."

"You had sweets and a SHOW? What show?" I ask.

"It wasn't that good. It was a play of some kind. You wouldn't have liked it, Tom," Derek assures me.

"Really?" I say before Marcus interrupts.

"Are you kidding? You would have loved it, Tom. The play was SO FUNNY. We were all LAUGHING a lot, weren't we?" Marcus asks everyone.

"Maybe a little," AMY says.

Ha! Ha! Ha! Ha!

The others try not to look like they enjoyed it too much.
Except Marcus, who keeps LAUGHING.

"Hey — someone put a picture of a dinosaur on the

PET NOTICEBOARD."

"Norman jumps up and ROARS!

AGGHHHHRRRR!

"What about the picture of two FURRY caterpillars
and a note saying they were Mr Keen's eyebrows?"

Marcus reminds everyone.

"Who did that?" I want to know.

"BUSTER JONES!" they all tell me.

"Honestly, Tom – apart from the show, the school trip, the sweets and the pet noticeboard, you haven't missed much," Derek says, trying to make me feel better.

"Oh ... we did beat the little kids at Champ."

"It only happened once," Derek says.

"Twice," Florence corrects him.

"I THINK we beat them three times. It doesn't happen often."

"That's because I wasn't playing, Marcus." I try and make a joke of it.

It all goes quiet for a moment, then Norman shouts, "Mrs Nap's got SIX TOES on one foot!"

(Random.)

But it gets everyone talking again.

"So apart from the school trip, winning at Champ, and Mrs Nap's six toes (I might need more details on this), I haven't missed much. What about your party, Leroy?" I check.

"I changed the date so you can come!" Leroy is happy about that, but not as happy as ME.

THAT'S THE BEST NEWS EVER!

"What have you been doing, Tom?" Leroy asks me. I have to think for a moment, then say,

"I've been keeping a NOTEBOOK of interesting stuff, drawing, making things out of foil and growing some mustard and cress." Which sounds a lot more impressive than...

"I've been watching Mr Akedo park his car, keeping an eye on the squirrels, doing a furry cat jigsaw and watching the bins get picked up on Monday."

Rooster chooses this moment to *RUN* around Norman...

TIMBER!

...who lifts up one of the crutches ... and falls over.

He's not hurt, but Rooster's
REALLY **LOUD** barking makes Delia come out again.

"Keep the noise down, will you?"

"Everybody WAVE at my sister,"
I say, because she L♡VES that.

(She doesn't.)

Seeing Delia's cheery face reminds me about her POSTER.

I really need to get it back before she notices it's gone.

Norman, who's still on the ground, says,

"Hey, Tom!

I nearly forgot - I brought you a
CARAMEL DOUGHNUT. It's in my bag."

"You did? LET ME HELP YOU UP," I say.

I'm cheering.

HOORAY HOORAY HOORAY

I'm going to TRY a

CARAMEL DOUGHNUT,

FINALLY!

Caramel
doughnut

Norman goes to his bag and brings
out a slightly squashed doughnut.
"It's been in my bag all day,"
Norman tells me, but I don't care.
Then for SOME REASON, Norman decides to
THROW the doughnut to me.

I'm good at catching...

But not as good as ROOSTER,

who thinks it's for him ...

... it is now.

One day, I will get to
try a caramel doughnut.

RANDOM NEW FRIEND FUN

Sort of

Every day my foot's getting better. (☺)

Today I noticed there's a timetable on the

fridge door of things I'm supposed to be doing.

Appointments at the doctor, finishing schoolwork – (☹)

that kind of thing.

There's a ☆ **STAR** next to a note that

says...

> FRANK – meeting ☆ (bringing son)
>
> RITA – out

Those are Mum and Dad's first names. Bringing "son"

– I wonder who that is? So I go and find out.

Mum tells me that Dad has a client coming to our

house.

"Mr Sky is bringing his son with him, and as I'm not

here, we're hoping you could keep him company?"

137

"Oh, OK,"

I say, as this is a bit unexpected.

"You two can hang out together. It'll be nice to make a new friend, won't it?" Mum tells me.

 "Great – we can watch TV,"

I say (because that would be fun).

"OR ... he might be able to help you with your worksheets, Tom. That would be good, wouldn't it?"

"Not really. I'm sure he'd much rather watch TV. In fact, I should go and see what's on right now," I suggest.

"OK – I'm going to work, so promise me you'll look after Mr Sky's son.
He's a very important client for your dad.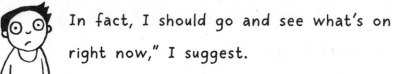
It would be so helpful, Tom."

(I get the message, Mum.)

"Sure, he'll be fine with ME. No need to worry. What's his name?" I want to know.

"His name's Bright and your dad says you two have a lot in common."

"Do we?" I say, hoping he'll like the same TV programmes as me.

I go and get comfy on the sofa and then realize this kid's name is Bright Sky.

Maybe he likes 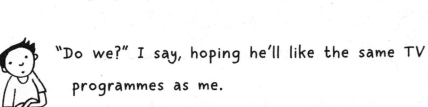 or caramel wafers too.

(Who doesn't like wafers?)

When the doorbell goes, Dad answers it, and it suddenly becomes clear <u>what</u> it is we have in common...

"Tom, this is Mr Sky and his son, Bright. And
you've **both** been in the wars," Dad says, and I
can see we've both got plaster casts – only his is on
his arm. Bright waves – with his good arm.

"How long before that comes off, Tom?" Mr Sky asks me.

"AGES," I tell him.

"Bright's due to have his cast taken off next week. Aren't you, Bright?" He nods.

Bright is peering out from under a lot of curly hair. He seems quite shy and doesn't say much.

"Let's get you two a snack while we have our meeting in the shed," Dad tells us both.

(This is a promising start.)

"Can we have the secret biscuit tin from your shed, Dad?" I ask straight away.

"No need to worry about Bright, we've brought our OWN food," says Mr Sky, holding up a Tupperware box.

"Biscuits?" I ask.

"No, Tom, just healthy snacks. Bright doesn't have any allergies ... but he's not allowed junk food,"

Mr Sky tells me.

This is very disappointing for me.

"Sure, no problem," Dad says.

 "**W**e should do more of that. No more wafers for you, Tom!" Dad jokes.

(I don't LAUGH.)

"Just help yourself to whatever you're allowed to have, Bright. We won't be long in the shed. You can watch TV with Tom," Dad suggests helpfully.

 "Actually, I'd rather he didn't watch TV during the day. But Bright's brought some games to play."

"I like games," I say, so it doesn't feel awkward.

Bright doesn't say anything. I wait until Dad and Mr Sky leave, then ask him a question. "Hey, Bright, what do you want to do then?"

He shrugs his shoulders. "I don't mind."

He seems like a nice, easy-going kid.

"What school do you go to?" I want to know.

"Great Manor," he says. (Of course he does.)

 "What happened to your arm?" I ask.

"I was climbing a tree and I fell out,"
he tells me.

 "Whoa, painful."

"What happened to your foot?" Bright asks me.

"Errrrrrm... I jumped off a high wall,"
I tell him, trying to make it sound more

DRAMATIC than the truth.

"Can we go to the kitchen, Tom?" he asks.

"Sure, follow me." I pick up my crutches to walk but

 Bright's *gone* already.

(143)

By the time I get to the kitchen, Bright is EATING OUT OF THE SUGAR BOWL! He's scooping spoonfuls of sugar straight into his mouth.

"What are you doing?" I ask him, even though I can <u>see</u> exactly what he's doing.

"Eating. It tastes amazing – thanks," Bright says and shoves in another spoonful.

"Do you always eat PLAIN sugar? I thought you weren't supposed to have that kind of thing," I check.

"I know – but it tastes yummy... Mmm..." Bright puts down the spoon and looks around for something else to eat. "What's in here?" he asks, opening a cupboard.

"Just cereal, tins, jam – that kind of thing," I explain.

"JAM – I LOVE jam!" Bright tells me.

"**STRAWBERRY! MY FAVOURITE!**"

Bright eats a great dollop of jam straight from the jar.

I have **GOT** to get him out of here!

"Let's go and watch TV, shall we?"

He takes one more spoonful, then follows me out to the hallway. There's <u>something</u> about our staircase that makes kids want to slide down it, and Bright's no different. He runs to the top ...

and, with his arm in a sling, still manages to

slide down FASTER than I've ever done.

WHEEEEEE

"Be careful!" I shout.

"That was **FUN**!" Bright says.

(Not for me, it wasn't.)

"Can I try a caramel wafer? I've never had one," Bright asks me.

I'm SHOCKED – but I'm sure he's not allowed. "I don't think we have any," I say, even though I'd quite like a wafer myself.

"Oh ... OK. I can do really good HANDstands – do you want to see?" Bright suddenly goes upside down and shows me. His foot BASHES a

picture of Delia and he knocks it on the ground.

"CLONK"

"Uh-oh..."

"Whoops!"

"Maybe you should come down – your face is going red," I tell him.

"Shall we go and hang out in your room, then?" he suggests. Before I can say YES ... he's already gone upstairs...

I follow as fast as I can, wondering HOW MUCH LONGER DAD'S MEETING IS GOING TO BE?!? When I get to my room, he's NOT there. I find him in DELIA'S ROOM!

"Don't go in THERE! That's my SISTER'S room!" I warn him, a little too late. He's already WEARING a pair of her sunglasses.

"These suit me – your sister has a LOT of sunglasses. Can I keep these?"

"Errrr, NO – Delia wouldn't be happy."

He leaves – but then heads straight to my parents' bedroom and *THROWS* himself on to their bed.

THEN he tries Dad's hat on.

Suits me!

"Have you got any pets?"
Bright wants to know.

"I'm not allowed pets – my sister's allergic," I say.

"Where's your room?" he asks.

"It's over..." But Bright leaves before I can finish.

I go after him.

(Bright is WILDER than Norman on sugar – only worse.)

"Can I draw on your blackboard? I'm not that good at drawing," he says and SCRIBBLES all over my monster.

"Oops, sorry, I've snapped your chalk," Bright tells me. (Luckily I have more.)

"What's under your bed?" he wants to know NOW. He drags out some of my favourite **comics.**
"Oh, the Jolly Fruit Bunch – I like them! Can I keep this to read later?" Bright asks me.

I take a deep breath. I've read it before, so I say, "Fine, you can keep it," thinking that will be the END of it.

 "Thanks, Tom," Bright says. "You've got a lot of cool stuff in your bedroom," he adds, looking around.

 "WOW – this crisp packet badge is amazing," he says, picking one up.

"YES, it is. I make them myself," I tell him.

"Can I have this one?" he asks.

(Bright won't stop asking for things.)

 "No, that's a special badge," I say.

"Oh... I thought you had a lot of them."

Bright puts it back.

This kid is driving me mad now.

I need to get him back downstairs.

"I just REALLY like that badge.

I'd never be able make one like that."

"Shall we go and watch some TV?" I suggest.

He sighs really loudly and agrees, then runs out, leaving "his" **comic** behind. Maybe he didn't want it after all.

I really hope DAD FINISHES SOON!

By the time I get to the front room, Bright's already sitting on the sofa with the remote control. He's turning the TV ON and OFF and ON and OFF. I take the remote away and put on the **Jolly Fruit Bunch**. For a few moments, Bright seems to calm down, and we're both enjoying the show – until Mr Sky comes in ...

... and turns OFF the TV.

"Come on, Bright. You know you're not supposed to watch TV during the day," Mr Sky tells him.

"It was Tom's idea," Bright says, a bit *QUICK* to blame me.

Sounds like you, Tom!

Dad LAUGHs

and guides Mr Sky and Bright to the door.
"Thank you for coming round – I'll have that project sorted for you next week,"

I hear him saying. I'm pleased they're leaving too.

"**I** forgot my **COMIC!**" Bright tells us, and runs upstairs to grab it.

"What do you say, Bright?" Mr Sky asks.

"Can we go?" Bright answers.

"No, Bright – what ELSE do you say?"

"Can we go NOW ... please?" Bright says, and his dad tries again.

"Oh yes – thanks for having me," Bright tells me and Dad, then they head off. We watch them go.

"Thanks for keeping Mr Sky's son company, Tom. He seems like a really nice boy. Right – better get back to work."

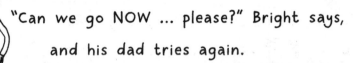

Before I get the chance to tell Dad about the sugar bowl, the jam or how Bright tried on his HAT, Dad goes back to work in the shed.

It's been a very tiring morning, so I go back to watching TV. I get the chance to put my foot UP and rest.

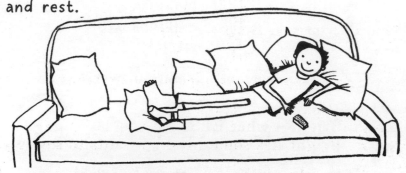

I'm busy watching my second episode of **Jolly Fruit Bunch** when the doorbell goes. WHO'S THAT? As Dad's in the shed, I go and answer it. I'm not expecting to see Mr Sky and Bright back again, but there they are – and Mr Sky looks cross. Has Bright blamed **me** for him eating 𝕤𝕦𝕘𝕒𝕣? (I don't like the look of this.)

"My dad's in the shed – I'll go and get him," I say straight away.

"No, Tom – it's you I need to speak to," Mr Sky says sternly.

Uh-oh...

I start wobbling on my crutches.

It sounds like I'm in trouble.

"Bright has something he wants to say to you.

Don't you, Bright?" Mr Sky says.

Bright doesn't look like he wants to say anything –

So I get in first.

"It wasn't <u>MY</u> fault he ate 𝔖𝔲𝔤𝔞𝔯 from the

bowl, or jam from the jar, he just helped himself!"

Mr Sky looks surprised.

"Well <u>THAT</u> explains a lot.

Did you do that, Bright?"

"Maybe a little taste, Dad."

Then Bright holds out his good hand and says,

"I'm sorry I took this, Tom."

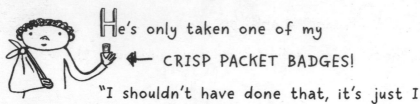 He's only taken one of my

→ CRISP PACKET BADGES!

"I shouldn't have done that, it's just I
REALLY love it. Sorry, Tom."

He does look sorry. I think he means it.

"I asked Bright where he got the badge from,
and he finally admitted he took it from your
room, Tom – so he's giving it back,"

Mr Sky tells me.

I think for a moment, then surprise myself by saying,

"Oh, that's OK. Don't you remember, Bright?
I said you could have the badge along with
the **comic.** I've got loads. He can keep it,
Mr Sky."

Mr Sky smiles at me.

"That's very kind of you, Tom, are you sure?

What do you say, Bright?"

"BRILLIANT!" he shouts.

"... Oh, and thanks so much."

He does seem really happy now and puts the badge back on.

I wave them goodbye just as Dad comes back in.

"Was that Mr Sky again? Did he forget something?"

"Yes – I gave Bright one of my crisp packet badges and he left it behind," I decide to say.

"That was very nice of you, Tom. Well done. He's a VERY important client, so I'm glad you and Bright got on so well."

"Sort of..." I say.

"I've got another meeting with him next week. Shall I ask him to bring Bright over again?" Dad asks me.

"NO THANKS, Dad," I say quickly.

Bright WORE me out.

RANDOM FUN WITH DELIA

← This is not a joke

TOM! Derek's here AGAIN!

Delia calls to me from downstairs. This is excellent and good timing as I'm hoping he's brought Delia's poster back from school for me. I want to tell him about Bright too. (What a kid.) Can I have it?

Derek comes upstairs to my room and we high-five.

"How's the ankle?"

"Still there..."

Then Derek says, "I have a SURPRISE!"

Straight away, I'm thinking...

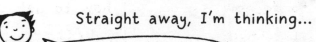 You have DOUGHNUTS!

But then he opens his bag and out pops...

ROOSTER, who runs around my room and makes himself comfy on Granny Mavis's knitted foot warmers.

"Good boy." I give him a cuddle, then close the door properly so he stays well away from Delia.

Derek has brought back Delia's poster as well. He unfolds it carefully for a last look. "I wish I had a SIGNED poster like this. We should do a **DOGZOMBIES** poster."

(I agree.)

I fold the poster up and put it back in the envelope to keep it safe and away from Rooster.

"All we have to do now is work out how to get the poster back in Delia's room without her knowing

  I took it,"

I tell Derek.

"Why don't you just wait until she leaves her room?" Derek asks.

"BECAUSE ... the longer that poster is in my room, the more likely it is Delia will find it. She just <u>KNOWS</u> stuff without me saying anything. I don't know how," I explain.

Then suddenly there's a knock at my door.

KNOCK! KNOCK! KNOCK!

"Is Rooster with you again, Tom?"
It's Delia.

"No..." I answer.

"I know he is - keep him in there, please," she snaps, then goes back to her room.

"See what I mean? She <u>knows</u> things," I say to Derek. "How does she do it?"

"And HOW are we going to get the poster back in her room now?" Derek wants to know.

It's a good question.

"We could make a BIG distraction and keep her busy," I suggest.

 "What kind of a distraction?"

"I don't know - let's have a think."
We sit on the edge of my bed and try to come up with something clever. Derek has an idea.

 "I could keep her talking about BANDS and  downstairs while you SNEAK in?"

"I'm a bit noisy walking right now. She'd hear me - and talking about would only remind her about the poster,"
I tell Derek.

"Good point."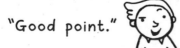

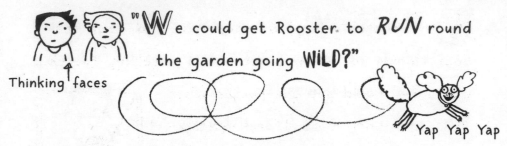

Yap Yap Yap

"I've just said Rooster's not here, she'll be really cross."

"How about I make her a cup of tea and a wafer and give it to her downstairs? Then you could sneak into her room."

"But if I'm in her room putting the poster back, what happens if she brings her tea UPSTAIRS?"

Derek points out.

AGH!

"I'll keep her talking, and if that doesn't work – I'll fall over."

We agree this is the BEST idea so far and it involves wafers, so it's a win-win situation.

With Rooster asleep, we sneak out and close the door tightly so he can't get out. I'm telling Derek where he should put the poster when Delia opens her door. Derek quickly hides the poster behind his back.

"What do you two want?"

"Would you like a cup of tea and a wafer, Delia?" I say while Delia views me with SUSPICION.

"Who are you and what have you done with my brother?" she says, not smiling.

 "I'm making tea for Mum, Dad and Derek."

"I love tea and wafers," Derek says, backing me up.

"No thanks, Tom, I'm OK."
She goes back in her room and closes the door.

(She wasn't supposed to do that.)

PLAN B

We're going to pretend someone's at the door to get Delia to come downstairs while Derek puts the poster back in her room.

"I won't have much time," Derek points out.

"I know – but I have an even better idea." So while Derek goes upstairs to get ready, I find an old box and write Delia's name on it. (I try <u>not</u> to make it look like my handwriting.) Then I quietly open the door and put the parcel on the doorstep.

"Delia, there's a parcel down here for you!" I shout and RING the doorbell. It's the wrong way around, but it does the trick.

Delia shouts back, "Be down in a minute."

(So far so good.)

Suddenly Mum appears and PICKS UP the parcel!

"Is this for Delia? I'll take it up to her,"

she tells me, then closes the door and heads upstairs.

Awwwww, NO – THAT wasn't supposed to happen.

PLAN C

I go to tell Derek what happened, as he's still waiting with the poster to run into Delia's room.

"Plan B didn't work – we need a Plan C," I explain.

"What shall we do now?" Derek wants to know.

"We WAIT – she'll have to go out soon," I say, when there's a knock on my door.

KNOCK   (Oh no...)

KNOCK

KNOCK

"TOM, WHY DID YOU SEND ME AN EMPTY BOX?"

It's Delia and she's woken up Rooster too.

He's running round my bedroom with a foot warmer on his head.

"Erm... It must be a mistake. It wasn't me," I tell her VERY unconvincingly.

"YEAH, RIGHT. AND I KNOW ROOSTER'S IN YOUR ROOM. JUST KEEP HIM UNDER CONTROL, WILL YOU?"

I look at Derek and whisper,

"I told you she knows STUFF. He's NOT here, Delia!"

I shout back.

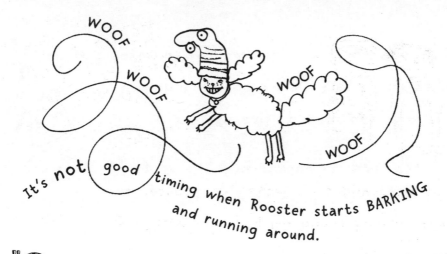

WOOF WOOF WOOF WOOF

It's not good timing when Rooster starts BARKING and running around.

"Oh ... here he is. Good boy, Rooster!"

I try and cover up.

"I'm not stupid, Tom. Have you taken my DuDE3 poster? I can't find it,"

Delia wants to know.

"What poster?"

I stall for time. Delia is sneezing now.

"Just keep Rooster away from me, please,"

she says.

"I think I'd better go," Derek says.

He puts Rooster in his bag (which takes a while), then hands back Delia's poster and wishes me luck, and we high-five.

Derek heads home and now it's up to <u>ME</u> to work out **HOW** I'm going to get this poster back into Delia's room without her finding out.

I think of a few different ideas.

Some are better than others.

poster

In the end I decide there's only ONE thing I can do.

I have to tell the truth.

I need to let her know that I took  (borrowed) her poster for my **SHOW AND TELL.**

Fingers crossed, she won't be too mad at me.

Here goes.

GULP

I **KNOCK** on her door and wait.

And wait...

(Nothing.)

So I knock again.

"Delia ... it's TOM.

I've got something for you."

(Silence.)

"Rooster's gone and I've got your poster here. I'm sorry – I should have asked you ... but ... it was my **SHOW AND TELL.** I wanted to bring the poster into my class to tell them about **DUDE 3**. But then I had my accident, and it was still at school. So I've only just got it back."

I stop and listen at the door.

"Delia?"

I knock on the door again in case she didn't hear me.

KNOCK! KNOCK!

"I **AM** sorry for taking your poster ... Delia?"

Maybe she's got headphones on and can't hear me. I open the door very slowly and peer into her room. I'm expecting to see Delia GLARING at me from behind her glasses,  but the room's EMPTY.

This is ✰BRILLIANT✰.

I can put back the poster where I found it and pretend it was there all the time.

PLAN D WORKED AFTER ALL!

YES!

Mission complete! I go back to my room and add the **DUDE3** logo to my plaster cast in celebration.

That was a VERY LUCKY ESCAPE! :)

We haven't had a **DOGZOMBIES** band practice for **AGES**. It's not the same, but I try and write a song about what's been happening to me and my foot, and how I've been trying to make the best of things and having as much fun as I can

(under the circumstances).

It's called...

RANDOM ACTS of FUN

and it goes like this ... ➡️

FUN...

RANDOM ACTS of FUN

A song by ME – Tom Gates

Hey, little bug

You need a holiday

Pack up your bag

And head for the

SUPER-FUN HIGHWAY

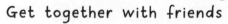

Get together with friends

You've travelled for miles

Welcome to FUNLAND

Where everyone smiles

Do RANDOM things

 Draw a giraffe

Make up a dance

Have a good laugh

 Eat carrots for breakfast

Sing in the rain

Make up a joke

Then tell it again

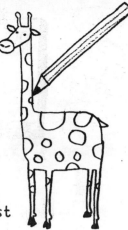

 Every day's a FUN day

Even on a Monday

Have a really good day

FUN is coming your way

RANDOM FUN
with the
COUSINS

I'm getting a bit bored of sitting around the house now. So when the cousins come round for a visit, I'm EXTRA happy to see them.

"We brought you some   from that **Bakery**," they tell me.

(That gets me excited.)

"REALLY? THANKS SO MUCH!"

"But we ate them on the way over."

Mmmm   Mmmm

"They were AMAZING."

"Oh ..."

"Sorry - it's the thought that counts, right?"

they tell me.

 "I suppose so..."

"And we DID think of you when we ate them."

"Thanks for letting me know."

The cousins point to my crutches that are

leaning up against the wall.

(I'm trying not to use them so much.)

"Can we have a go?" they ask.

"Sure - but let's go outside in case you

knock something over."

(Like me.)

— My turn.

By the time I make it outside, the cousins are already taking it in turns to see how *FAST* they can get round the garden using my crutches. It's not as easy as they thought it would be.

"Hello, you two. Slow down, will you? We don't want any more broken bones around here!" Dad says, but the cousins take no notice.

"How's your mum and dad?" he asks.

"Fine, apart from Dad — his feet really hurt," they tell Dad.

"What's wrong – did he drop his wallet on them?"
Dad asks, LAUGHING at his own joke.

"No, he went hiking in his BRAND-new
walking boots and got really bad blisters."

 "That sounds like my brother. Has he been using
his METAL DETECTOR again?"
Dad asks, just as the cousins get carried away and
topple into the flower bed.

Then Dad suggests we watch TV,
which suits me fine.

There's a show on called HIDDEN TREASURES.
Mum and Dad **love** this programme.

It's where people show different objects to an EXPERT →  to find out more about them and how much they are worth. There was one episode where someone used a metal detector and found a whole chest of **TREASURE** that was worth a **FORTUNE.** Uncle Kevin and the cousins saw it too. The cousins asked for metal detectors for their birthday after that. Seeing **HIDDEN TREASURES** on TV reminds me of their birthday.

Uncle Kevin bought three metal detectors (one each for the cousins' birthday and one for him). He arranged for us to go to a field to try them out.

BEEP

He let ME use his detector, so I could have a go as well, although he stood behind me most of the time and pointed out all the places I should be looking.

Very quickly, I found ... an old key, some coins (not old), and a badge ← I really liked.

No **treasure**, though.

"Let's divide up the space and each take a small section – we don't want to keep going over the same parts of the field," Uncle Kevin suggested.

He was taking it all VERY seriously.

After another HOUR, none of us had found anything. (Just junk.)

We were all getting a bit bored and the detectors were getting heavy to hold.

So Uncle Kevin STEPPED in and said he wanted to have a go now.

"Look and learn, kids! We won't be going home empty-handed. I'll find something – you'll see," he told us, like we hadn't been doing it properly.

Uncle Kevin moved the detector round and the sound went OFF really loudly.

BEEP
BEEP
BEEP

"Right, this might be worth digging up," he said and went to the car to get his shovel. We all watched as Uncle Kevin began to dig. "Stand back, boys – let's see what's down there."

When he found nothing, he picked up the detector again and waved it around.

The **BUZZING** was still REALLY LOUD.

"There's something good down there – I can tell,"
Uncle Kevin told us. "Just got to be patient..."
he added and began to dig again.

But nothing seemed to be there.

"I'm not giving up, boys. You can wait in the car,"

he told us.

"It's taking a long time to find the **treasure**,"

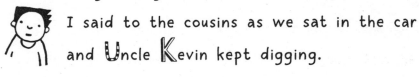 I said to the cousins as we sat in the car
and Uncle Kevin kept digging.

"Can we GO HOME now? We're HUNGRY,"
the cousins shouted through the windows.

"It will be worth it, boys. I've never heard a
metal detector go off like that!"

It was starting to get dark...

Then Uncle Kevin walked over to the car ... and turned on the headlights so he could see better.

Won't be long NOW!

Uncle Kevin kept on digging until two hours later, when he gave up and put the metal detector back in the car boot.

Next time.

BEEP

BEEP

BEEP

He drove me home and Dad opened the door as we walked up the path.

"You're back LATE! What did you find? Are we celebrating?" he asked, cheerily.

"Nothing YET, but I nearly found something BIG," Uncle Kevin was keen to say.

"We had fun though, didn't we, Tom?"

I nodded.

"No treasure, then? That's a shame,"

Dad asked me.

"No, but Uncle Kevin was digging for hours and WOULDN'T give up," I told Dad.

"I'll go back tomorrow. Something's there," Uncle Kevin told Dad, who looked down at his boots and said,

"Dressed for the part as ever, Kevin."

"You know me, Frank. I like to do things properly. Better go – I can see my boys are looking for treats in the glove compartment," he added.

Uncle Kevin headed back quickly.

Dad and I waved them goodbye as they drove OFF.

"That's the funniest thing EVER," he said, LAUGHING.

"What's so FUNNY?"
I asked.

"Was the metal detector going off every time Kevin picked it up?" Dad wants to know.

"YES! It was BUZZING like mad."

"Well, THAT'S what happens when you wear STEEL-CAPPED boots and hold a metal detector near your feet!"
Dad just about got his words out.

"Are you going to tell him?" I wondered.

"He'll work it out ... eventually!"
Dad was really enjoying this.

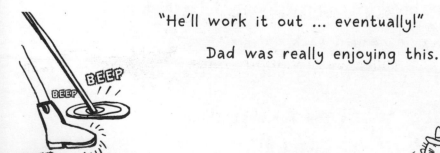

Even now, Dad sometimes likes to ask
Uncle Kevin about the metal detector
and the **treasure** he <u>never</u> found.
Uncle Kevin pretends nothing
happened.

It's funny how watching **HIDDEN TREASURES**
on TV reminded me of Uncle Kevin's steel-capped
boots! I don't think the cousins know anything about
them. I bet Uncle Kevin kept it quiet.

"What do you want to watch, then?" I ask them.
They take the remote and flick channels.

"This looks good."

It's a show called Tiny Vampire Bats.  small

(I hope it's not scary.)

YUM

No need to worry –
Tiny Vampire Bats
is a lot funnier
than expected...

YUM YUM

Tiny vampire, big teeth

Random Paint FUN

I LOVE the paint set that Granny Mavis and Granddad Bob gave me. I've been testing the colours and trying to use the different brushes, while painting nice pictures of ALL kinds of things.

Here's Derek looking surprised

Derek surprised

(189)

Here's a **POSTER** I painted of DELIA when I couldn't find the LAST piece of my FLUFFY CAT jigsaw. I SUSPECTED she'd hidden it – and I was RIGHT! I found it stuck on the fridge with a smiley face magnet.

How annoying was that? (Very.)

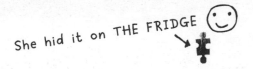

She hid it on THE FRIDGE

WANTED
Jigsaw ThieF
Extra ANNOYING

Here's a nice picture of Marcus.

Some perky blueberries

A jolly sprout

Nice smiling strawberry

A blob monster

Pesky dog

When Granny and Granddad POP round they are really impressed with my paintings.

"These are GREAT, TOM! Do you want to come with us for a change of scene? Bring your paints – it's the perfect place to practise painting different people," Granddad tells me.

"I'm OK here, thanks," I say, because I guess they're going to the LEAFY GREEN OLD FOLKS' HOME to see their friends, which won't be that much fun for me.

"Oh, that's a shame, Tom – we've been invited for TEA and you could get a ride on our NEW mobility scooter too."

"I'll get my stuff."

(They had me at tea.)

THE FOSSILS have **UPGRADED**

their mobility scooter.

It's got a nice W I D E comfy seat for two.

Granny uses her skateboard to HITCH a ride,

which is OK so long as Granddad doesn't go

~~too~~ ~~c u~~ *FAST.*

We get to the LEAFY GREEN OLD FOLKS'

HOME at exactly the right moment (teatime).

Vera wants to know what happened to my FOOT.

"I did something silly," I say.

"I do silly things ALL the time," Vera tells me, then

pulls the trolley closer!

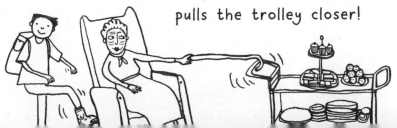

I'm about to tuck in when Granny Mavis tells
everyone, "Tom's passing round the sandwiches,
aren't you, Tom?"

Looks like I am.

"You should have been here yesterday, Tom,
we had the most delicious **DOUGHNUTS**
from the new **Bakery**," Vera tells me as
she helps herself to a cake.

"ARE YOU KIDDING ME?"
I MISSED OUT on the DOUGHNUTS
AGAIN!

Then Teacup Tony joins in the doughnut appreciation
fan club by saying, "It was the BEST
doughnut I've ever had in my whole life,
and I'm ninety-five years old."

(Only one of these things is true.)

I take a sandwich and some cake – but it doesn't taste the same now.

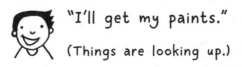 "Tom's been doing some lovely paintings. I've said he should paint some of **you** here, if that's OK?" Granny lets the whole of LEAFY GREEN OLD FOLKS' HOME know.

This wasn't EXACTLY what I had planned and if I'm honest I'd rather eat my cake.

Then Vera says, "You can paint me, Tom. I'll give you some pocket money to get yourself a doughnut if you want – just make me look FABULOUS!"

"I'll get my paints."

(Things are looking up.)

I start with Vera, who's a lot easier to paint than I expected ...

... especially as she's asleep.

Vera

Cake crumbs

Here's Teacup Tony

and Maurice

I don't wake Vera up. Instead, Granny and Granddad
give me some pocket money and I leave her the painting.

I know EXACTLY what I want to spend my money
on too...

Some carrots

A doughnut of course

THE FOSSILS' mobility scooter can't go fast enough for me.

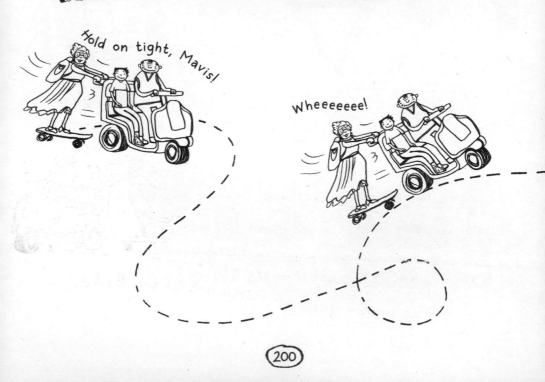

Hold on tight, Mavis!

Wheeeeeee!

Only it's closed.

(This isn't funny any more.)

The sign in the window says,

They're <u>not</u> as sorry as I am. :(

SLOW-GROWN FUN

Granny and Granddad take me home and try to get my mind off doughnuts by talking about other things. (It's not really working.)

"How's the mustard and cress growing, Tom?"

"It's alive and doing OK, thanks."

"Let's have a look, then. Maybe we can put some in a nice SANDWICH. It's not exactly a doughnut, but you'll have the SATISFACTION of knowing you've grown it ALL yourself," Granddad tells me.

Which is true, but I'd still rather have a doughnut.

I go and get Delia-in-a-pot, and her hair looks pretty impressive now – but not as impressive as Mr Fullerman's, which is OUT OF CONTROL.

Mr Fullerman with green hair

"Let's give them both a TRIM!" Granny suggests and helps me to make cheese sandwiches with mustard and cress, my SECOND tea today.

They are surprisingly tasty for green stuff, but the FUNNIEST thing about growing my own food is...

The random green haircuts
Delia and Mr Fullerman have now.

(I'm definitely growing more mustard and cress.)

SHOW AND TELL
FUN (Finally)

After a VERY L O N G six weeks, I finally get my plaster cast taken OFF. I ask the doctor if I can keep it, so they are extra careful with the saw. (That's RIGHT, they use a small saw to cut it off my foot, which is exciting.) WOW

I am very BRAVE - unlike Dad,

who can't look.

I take the plaster cast home in a bag.

(I'm not going to lie - after six weeks on my foot, it does whiff a tiny bit.)

Please don't break any more bones, Tom.

Look, Dad! It's in here.

I tell everyone at breakfast that,
"I'm REALLY looking forward to going back
to school now my plaster cast is off."

"I feel the same way, Tom," Delia joins in.

(I ignore her.)

"And I've really missed my friends.
I wonder if they've missed me?" I say.

"OF **COURSE** they'll have missed you,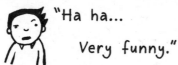
Tom - who wouldn't?" Mum tells me.

"ME..." Delia answers.

"Ha ha...

Very funny."

"You're going to have a great time, Tom.
Just be careful, won't you?" Dad says.
"No more broken bones!"

"Or jumping for doughnuts," Delia adds.

As if that's EVER going to happen again. ☺

Everyone seems very pleased to see me at school.
I'm glad to be back too!

Solid gives me a hug and lifts me off the ground. Even the little kids ask if I can play Champ with them at break time.

"We've missed beating you," they tell me.

"I'm not quite match-fit yet," I say, making my excuses early.

In class, Mr Fullerman thinks I did a good job keeping up with my work. **"We're all pleased to see Tom back with a mended foot,"** he says during registration.

I'm busy looking at the walls, which are filled with pictures of all the *FUN* things I've missed out on.

There seems to be a LOT more than my friends told me about.

Marcus and AMY welcome me back with a DOUBLE HIGH FIVE.

Marcus can't wait to tell me,

"I've got my OWN Venus flytrap now."

"Good for you, Marcus," I say.

"I've got one too," AMY adds.

(Another thing I've missed out on, then.)

 "Hey, Tom, are you going to do your
SHOW AND TELL today?" AMY asks.

"Yes, I AM!"

"What are you going to talk about then?"

Marcus wants to know.

"It will be a SURPRISE for you, Marcus."

"Have you <u>finally</u> got a pet, Tom?"

"How did you guess?" I say convincingly.

"It's in my bag now."

"What is it, then?"

I think for a moment and decide to have some FUN.

"A tiny vampire bat," I say.

A WHAT?

Marcus seems **shocked.**

"I'll get it out. I think it's hungry," I tell him.

"What does it eat?" Marcus says, moving away.

"It loves to BITE boys with curly hair."

"Don't be stupid, Tom." Marcus looks nervous.

**"Tom, are you ready to do your
SHOW AND TELL for the class?"**

Mr Fullerman wants to know.

"YES I AM, SIR!"

"Tom's brought in his tiny vampire bat, sir!" Marcus shouts.

Only, he's wrong.

It's my plaster cast.

I asked to save it so I could bring it into school.
I talk all about the different doodles, everyone
who's signed it and how it reminds me of all the
things that have happened over the last six weeks.

"Well done, Tom. That was an excellent SHOW AND TELL and a lesson for everyone NOT to jump up too high while holding a caramel doughnut,"

Mr Fullerman tells the class when he really doesn't need to. But he gives me ...

TWO MERITS,

which is a BRILLIANT

start to my week back at school. ☺

And it's going to get EVEN BETTER, because after school some of my friends want to go to the Bakery so I can finally get to taste one of those

CARAMEL DOUGHNUTS.

I think it's a VERY good idea.

I CAN'T WAIT!

Mmmmmmmmm

(But I have to, as I've still got a whole day of school left...)

Marcus keeps asking me about tiny vampire bats.

I wish I hadn't mentioned it now.

Exactly how big are they, then?

It was a joke, Marcus.

Tiny...

Derek, Marcus and **AMY** are all coming to the **Bakery** with me.

"This is **IT**, Tom, your doughnut moment has arrived!" Derek reminds me.

"I'm really looking forward to TASTING the gooey caramel, the fluffy inside with the delicious topping..." I say, making everyone hungry.

We walk round the corner and the **Bakery** is in sight.

Marcus shouts,

"CAN YOU SEE WHAT I CAN SEE?"

A group of GREAT MANOR school kids are already there and walking <u>INTO</u> the **Bakery!**

OH NO! NOT AGAIN!

"We should *RUN!*" Marcus tells me.

"It's not far – let's GO!" AMY agrees.

I don't want to trip up, so I say, "Hold on – we're going to be OK. Let's keep calm and do fast walking instead."
Then we all break into a very speedy stroll that gets faster and *faster* and more <u>TENSE</u> the closer we get.

I push open the door just in time ...

... to hear the shopkeeper say,

"These are the LAST

we've got, all for you."

"NO!" I shout.

"I told you we should have *RUN!*"
Marcus tells us, unhelpfully. We're too late — the last
caramel doughnuts are already in a bag and being
handed over to the Great Manor kids, who turn
around and SMILE at us.

I recognize one kid.

It's only **BRIGHT SKY**, who's wearing
the crisp packet badge I gave him.

"Tom! What are you doing here?" he asks.
"Not buying a caramel doughnut, by the looks of it.
You've got the **LAST ONES,**" I say in a
disappointed voice, because I <u>AM</u> very disappointed.
Bright opens the bag and hands me a 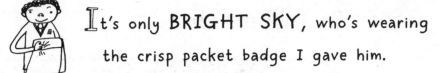.

"Here, have this one. Thanks for not getting
me into trouble about your badge. I OWE you," he
tells me.

"REALLY?" I ask, just in case he's joking
                  (like my sister does).

"I'll have it if Tom doesn't want it!" Marcus says.
"No chance. I'll take it. Thanks, Bright," I tell him
before he changes his mind.

"Enjoy your first caramel doughnut – and don't
        tell my dad I was here!" he adds.
"I will – I mean I won't tell your dad –
but I will enjoy the doughnut."

It's everything I dreamed of.

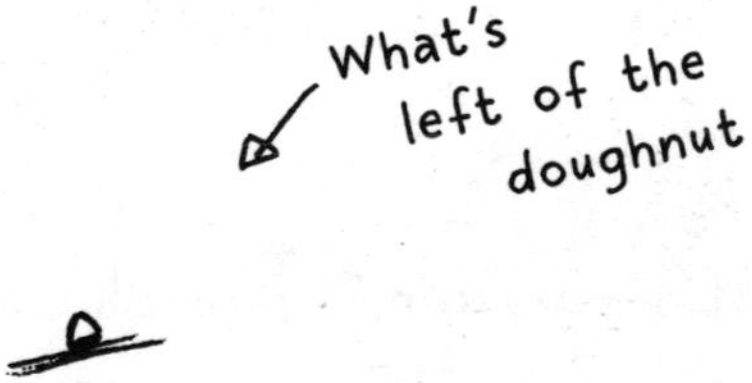

What's
left of the
doughnut

I'm still on cloud nine from the taste of the CARAMEL DOUGHNUT.

Derek, AMY and Marcus got jam doughnuts instead, which were nice – but not as good as <u>my</u> caramel one.

"Is Bright the kid who ate from the sugar bowl?" Derek asks me.

"He's the one."

"That's random," Derek says.

"See you at school tomorrow, Tom! Great to have you back. Band practice at mine, right?" he checks.

"Of COURSE! I've got a new song to play you,"
I tell him.

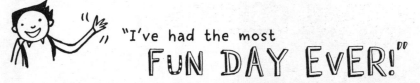

At home, Dad asks me how my day went.

"I've had the most

FUN DAY EVER!"

I tell him, happily. Then Dad says,

"Your sister was looking for you.

She's left something in your bedroom."

Which doesn't sound good and spoils what

<u>WAS</u> a really good day.

"Oh ... what's she doing in <u>MY</u> bedroom?"

I want to know.

"I think you'll be PLEASED," Dad tells me.

I'm not so sure.

I go to my room and open the door ... slowly.

Delia's bound to have done something

ANNOYING or I'm in trouble about something.

There's a message on my blackboard that says...

TOM

This signed
poster is
for YOU.
It's the one YOU
took from my
room without asking me.
(YES, I knew all along.)
It was ALWAYS for you, but
you spoiled the surprise because
you are a DOUGHNUT.
(Ha!)
Love from your brilliant, kind
sister Delia xx
PS Don't take things from my room again.

I take it back.

My sister has only given me the **DUDE 3** poster after all.

I don't think this day can get any better.

(Apart from if I got a pet.)

I am also a very nice brother and I give Delia one of my favourite badges, because I know how much she loves my crisp packet collection.

(She'd better wear it.)

Still full

Random
doughnut
bug

Ha Ha

How to make a FOIL CUP

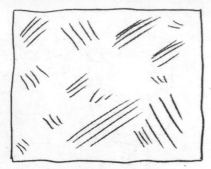

1. Take a piece of foil – recycled is perfect.

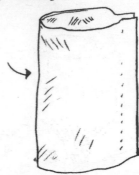

2. Fold in half.

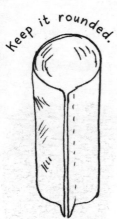

Keep it rounded.

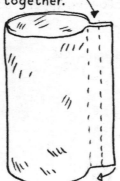

Put the edges together.

Fold the ends over twice to secure ...

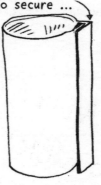

Now fold the TOP over and smooth the edge out.

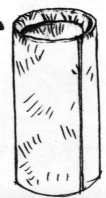

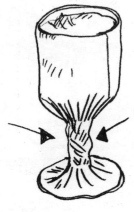

PUSH the foil IN to create a stem.

Use your fingers to MOULD the foil into a cup shape.

Press the base of the top down gently, so it stands up.

(You can also use foil wrappers as well.)

CONGRATULATIONS!
10 MERITS
FOR YOU!

Here's one I made earlier →

And the mystery bird on page 100 was ... a parakeet!

EVEN MORE B**OO**ks

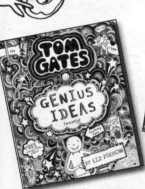

www.thebrilliantworldoftomgates.com
www.lizpichon.com

Liz Pichon is one of the UK's best-loved and bestselling creators of children's books. Her TOM GATES 😊 series has been translated into 45 languages, sold millions of copies worldwide, and has won the Roald Dahl Funny Prize, the Blue Peter Book Award for Best Story and the younger fiction category of the Waterstones Children's Book Prize.

In the ten years since THE BRILLIANT WORLD OF TOM GATES first published, the books have inspired the nation's children to get creative, whether that's through reading, drawing, doodling, writing, making music or performing.

"I wanted to FILL the books with ALL the things I loved doing when I was a kid. It's just the best feeling ever to know children are enjoying reading the books, because I love making them. So thank you so much for choosing Tom Gates and keep reading and doodling!"

Visit Liz at www.lizpichon.com

(School photo of Liz being grumpy)